The Gl

Devecheaux Antiq

Book Four

By M.L. Bullock and A.E. Chewning

If this world is wearing thin
And you're thinking of escape
I'll go anywhere with you
Just wrap me up in chains
But if you try to go out alone
Don't think I'll understand
Stay with me
Stay with me
In the silence of your room
In the darkness of your dreams
You must only think of me
There can be no in-betweens
When your pride is on the floor
I'll make you beg for more
Stay with me
Stay with me
You'd better hope and pray
That you make it safe
Back to your own world
You'd better hope and pray
That you'll wake one day
In your own world
'Cause when you sleep at night
They don't hear your cries
In your own world
Only time will tell
If you can break the spell
Back in your own world
Stay with me
Stay with me

Stay, stay with me ahh-haaa
Stay, stay, stay, stay, stay
~ Shakespeare's Sister. 1992

Chapter One—Patrice

The room was filled with an array of people from all walks of life. An advertisement in the local magazine, *Lagniappe*, had caught my eye, and I couldn't resist checking it out. It seemed like just the thing I needed to sort out all the paranormal events that were surrounding our family. I did a quick head count. Wow! At least fifty people had assembled to hear tonight's guest.

I thought about inviting my sister, but Aggie was so consumed with honing her abilities that she wasn't too approachable at the moment. Which was fine, because this journey needed to be my own if I was ever going to completely understand it. Just because I won a few pageants in high school, my little sister believed I could do anything without any effort at all. Like my parents, Aggie thought I was perfect. The perfect sister, daughter and student. Nobody really knew me.

I was anything but perfect. But I let them believe what they wanted; that way, they felt better about life. They didn't know me at all. Not really. I didn't even know myself.

I found my way to an empty seat in the front row next to a middle-aged woman. Her hair was neatly pinned up into a bun, and her clothes were pressed to perfection. She looked up slightly from her spiral notebook and gave me a decent smile, which I returned, but she quickly turned back to her writing as soon as I sat down.

Not too friendly. Only in a superficial way.

I glanced around. I knew this crowd. Very superficial. The best of Mobile's high society. I looked over the pamphlet that had been handed out at the door. *Paranormal Society of Mobile – The Occult.*

Interesting font. The words were printed in big bold letters across the folded paper. There was a guest speaker tonight, Philip Arnaud, which was why all of us were here, I supposed.

I shifted in my seat as the lights dimmed. The stage lights came up, and standing there at the podium was the epitome of tall, dark and handsome. I drew a breath as he stepped fully into the spotlight. He looked like someone who'd stepped out of time, despite his modern clothing. His tight shirt left nothing to the imagination. Every ripple of his muscled arms showed through. My body flushed with heat, and I was thankful the theater house was dark. The stiff, proper woman beside me relaxed too, and I saw her briefly cross her legs.

Philip Arnaud smiled at the gathering, showing perfectly white teeth.

Get a grip, Patrice.

"Good evening, ladies and gentlemen." He spoke with a slight accent that I couldn't quite make out. European, maybe French? His voice was smooth and alluring. And strangely familiar. He continued, "My name is Philip Arnaud. I'm sure most of you have heard of me by now, but for those few seekers who are new, bienvenue to the world of the occult and paranormal."

The audience offered soft but steady applause. I clapped along with them. I couldn't take my eyes off of him. His jet-black hair matched his shirt. The only bit of color anywhere on him were his piercing green eyes.

"The world is full of differing opinions regarding the paranormal and the occult." Philip took a few steps away from the podium. "Some people are under the impression that we live our lives, day to day, with nothing spectacular around us. Nothing otherworldly. Those people are lost, confused and just plain uninteresting."

He paused, a sly grin spreading across his face, waiting for the laughter to die down. "But you, hungry pursuers of the truth, are the ones that walk with your eyes open. There are monsters, spirits and evil all around us, ladies and gentlemen. Sometimes, these things are closer than you think."

His eyes shifted toward me and paused. For a moment, the people around me faded into the darkness. Their faces blurred, and a buzzing sound filled my ears. I held my breath and waited.

For what? I had no clue.

Philip's easy smile warmed me, and I tore my eyes away. I stared at my hands briefly, and he continued, "If you are here, I would assume that you have had some dealings with the occult and your curiosity has gotten the better of you. I was just like you once, amazed and curious about this mysterious world. The darkness, the unknown. It's alluring in a way that nothing else on this earth has ever been or will ever be. Who here has had a touch of the unexplained enter their lives recently?"

I slowly raised my hand, along with at least a dozen other people around the room.

"How did it make you feel? Fearful? Excited? A mixture of strange emotions?" All of us nodded our heads in agreement.

Philip leaned against the podium. "Well, it is good that you are here." He winked and nodded in my direction. I felt my shoulders draw down, and I released a breath that traveled up from the pit of my stomach. Something I had been holding in for a long time. Some of my fear disappeared. "I am delighted to meet you. Delighted to help you along your journey."

His face softened, and his green eyes lowered as his hands patted the wooden podium. "I'm here with you tonight to tell you, dear wanderer, that you are not alone. That there are many like us out there who have experienced something we just can't quite explain. Like I said before, you have come to the right place. There is darkness out there—I've seen it with my own eyes. Felt it. Lived it. And have lost many people that were close to me because of it."

Philip's voice trailed off into legends of vampires, werewolves, and other creatures of the night. His voice was soothing and easy to listen to. I drifted in and out of the lecture, thinking about all of the things I had experienced in the last several months. And strangely enough, I didn't feel alone in my thoughts. Many times, Philip smiled in my direction and the hair on the back of my neck stood up. I shook my head slightly as the speech ended. Where had the time gone?

"I know that's a lot of information to take in for one night, and so, I'll leave you with this, ladies and gentlemen. Look around you, always look around you. Because darkness can hide in plain sight."

The room fell into an eerie silence as he glanced around. Philip continued, "And on that note, I'll be in the lobby to meet with anyone who would like to learn more about those things that go bump in the night." Laughter filled the theater. This guy really knew how to work a room. Philip lowered the mic on the podium and clasped his hands in front of him. "Merci beaucoup. Thank you very much for your time."

No, there didn't seem to be an insecure bone in his perfect body.

Like the rest of the hungry audience, I stepped into the lobby to meet the man of the hour. I waited awkwardly as the crowd surrounded him. Finally, they began to leave, their elegant shoes tapping the marble floor as they stepped out into the dark and muggy Mobile night.

It's now or never.

Chapter Two—Patrice

"Mr. Arnaud." I stepped forward and firmly placed my hand out in front of me. "I'm Patrice Kelly."

He shook my hand. "Patrice, what a lovely name."

"Thank you." I cleared my throat and glanced around. *What do I say now? Hey, I think I'm a psychic?*

"Did you enjoy the lecture?" he asked politely.

"Yes, actually, I found it really interesting. I do have some questions, though. Is there any way that we could chat? Maybe after your fan club leaves?" I glanced behind me. Oh, goodness. Where had these folks come from? They were not the crowd that was here before. Not at all. I didn't recognize any of them. Most were elegantly dressed in black. None of them looked at me directly.

"I have another engagement tonight, but perhaps you could attend my lecture tomorrow night at the University? It will be a little more in-depth and intimate. We would certainly have a chance to talk together then. Perhaps afterward?"

"Intimate?" I asked, blushing at the thought of being intimate with Philip. I could practically taste his lips.

"Yes, it is a much smaller crowd." Philip's smooth, pink lips parted into a turned-up grin. My cheeks warmed again. If I didn't know any better, I'd think he was reading my thoughts.

I brushed my hair behind my ear, trying to find the words. "No, I mean... Yes, I would love to attend. I'll definitely be there."

The words came out at a higher pitch than I'd planned, but they finally escaped my mouth. What was it about this guy? I was never one to stumble over my words with any man. Aggie usually put her foot in her mouth for both of us. Talking to guys came easily for me, but *not* with Philip Arnaud.

"Then it's settled. I'll see you tomorrow, and we can chat afterward. Does that sound good to you?"

I nodded my head quicker than I expected. "Yes, yes. It does." Gosh, I sounded like a little lost puppy. *Slow down, Patrice.*

"Bien, I'll see you tomorrow, Patrice. Here's my cell number in case something happens and you can't make it." Philip handed me a business card. It was black with red lettering, with only his name and number on it. "I would still like to be available to you."

"I am sure I will see you tomorrow night. I do not have any plans that I can think of. Good night."

"Good night, Patrice."

My wedged footsteps tapped across the floor and echoed through the lobby as I departed the building. Out of the corner of my eye, I saw the black-clad crowd circle Philip like a bevy of shiny black crows.

What an odd thought.

Philip Arnaud would be my little secret, for now. Aggie had enough on her plate, and maybe Philip could teach me how to protect my baby sister. That statue had turned out to be something more evil than any of us had ever expected. I refused to be in the dark any longer. I had to do something, learn more about what evil lurks out there and be prepared.

Before it was too late.

I couldn't get the reflection in the antique mirror out of my mind. The woman's sad eyes and longing stare. She was so lost and lonely. Her whispers echoed through my thoughts like a broken radio. I tried to put them out of my mind. Telling Aggie was not an option.

The only person I could turn to was Philip. He had become my confidant these past few weeks. We had a strange affinity for one another's company. We spent hours together, talking about the places he'd been, the things he'd seen. He was riveted by the antiques store and the strange things we'd encountered there. Philip encouraged me to dig deeper, to face my fear of the unknown. He was always so confident and unafraid.

My heart ached when we were not together. Philip had another lecture tonight. I could listen to him speak forever. His voice was so alluring, intelligent and poised, and his mere words put me at ease. Even his fan club, the mysterious ones in black, began to speak to me, to accept me. Lilian, Gray and Sebastian. They were not exactly friends of his, more like worshippers.

Aggie was the last person who needed to know about what I saw in the mirror. She had been so on edge recently. I'd speak to Philip tonight. He would know what I needed to do or not do. I trusted him fully.

Whether it was a good thing or a bad thing, he was like an addiction to me. Some might say an unhealthy one. For the first time in my life, I felt like I was finally doing something just for me.

My reflection stared back at me from the blank screen on my phone. I rubbed my thumb across it, lingering there for a moment.

Ding, ding.

"How did you know I was thinking of you?" I asked without a hello.

"That is my little secret," his silky voice responded. Visions of him kissing me filled my mind. And other things. Things I'd never done before.

His flirtatious demeanor made me shift in my seat. "Secrets, huh? I'm not sure I like secrets."

"I had a feeling. Call it a lover's intuition."

"Okay," I said with the excitement of a schoolgirl.

"I'm afraid I cannot meet you tonight. Something has come up of the utmost importance. Can we meet in a few days?"

My heart sank at his words. "Sure. I understand."

"Patrice, this is something I must do. I will have more information on that mirror as well. I must tend to this other issue. Speaking engagements are not as fluid as they seem. There's a lot of little details that have to be worked out prior to my arrival. I hope you understand."

"Of course," I reluctantly responded. "I said I understand. This gives me a little more time to get some things together for our meeting. I'll have the mirror too."

"Excellent," he responded after a moment of silence. In today's conversation, his accent was more pronounced. "I knew you'd understand. I'll see you soon."

The call disconnected without even a goodbye. I stared at the blank screen again, wondering what in the world I was getting myself into. This couldn't be healthy, this obsession with a man I barely knew. Exactly what did I know about him? I didn't know where he was from, although I knew he was well-traveled. I didn't know how old he was, although he had to be older than me.

None of that mattered anymore. I put the phone down and walked to my bedroom. I had to look in that mirror again. I wasn't going to wait for Philip. I had to see her face. Talk to her. Listen to her.

The skin on my hands crawled as I reached for it...

Chapter Three—Philip

I never tired of standing before a group of hungry mortals. I couldn't help but smile at the irony of it all, but there was no other way to describe them. Perhaps greedy. Greedy for power, greedy for knowledge. No matter how the more puritanical of mortals would like to argue that point, that had been my experience. There was always one soul in the crowd willing to do whatever it took to claim what I and a few others held. The power of life after death. And I had lots and lots of experience. Hundreds of years, as a matter of fact. Yes, these mortals had their motives; I could almost read their minds. With faces like sheep, blank and stupid, their minds were webs of intricacies, schemes, and plans. Except one.

Ah, Patrice was the exception. Yes, extremely rare is the uncluttered mind. The sweetness of her, of her blood and bones. They would be worth savoring, but my dead heart had other ideas. I longed for more than an easy meal or another predictable seduction.

Esmine! You have returned to me! I sensed the unique resonance of her soul. *Once, lifetimes ago, you loved me, Esmine. We stood on the walls of Atlantis and faced death together. The wave crushed us and swept our bodies away. Many times we'd missed one another, narrowly missed. But now I have found you again in this wild place. You do not remember me or our deep love. It's just as well because with your last breath, you cursed me, Esmine.*

And how I deserved those words.

"May you forever die, Philip. I love you no more." Esmine stared at her own reflection in the silver hand mirror, a gift from me. Her pale cheeks were growing colder by the second. Life was slipping out of her. The smell of blood, the blood of our unfortunate son, flooded my nostrils. He was gone already. Agony and hunger twisted together and accentuated my sorrow. Esmine could not see me. I relinquished my reflection, along with tears and my soul, when I made the Dark Trade.

There was no more hiding the truth from Esmine. And when she knew the truth, it disgusted her. Revulsion. I could see it on her face. The deformed child had been spirited away, but she could not "unsee" the result of our love. The baby's twisted body, his unusual hands and feet. I watched as she succumbed to Death's gnarled hand. She could not see me—my reflection was as empty as my own heart.

Soulless. Heartless. Empty. Extremely empty.

Even her spirit fled my presence. *No, I will not surrender you again, Esmine. I will keep you this time. I will keep you forever, and you will learn to love me again.* Our souls were tied together long ago.

"Mr. Arnaud," the man to my right said after clearing his throat.

I smiled, as was my response in any uncomfortable situation. Imagine being this age and feeling discomfort of any sort. With the help of the mirror, I will summon Esmine's spirit and bind her to this life. I will show Patrice no mercy. Patrice will die and Esmine will be born, finally.

Forever mine!

Yes, Philip! Forever yours! my clan whispered back to me. Their eyes glittered at me from the back of the room. They were practically invisible to these mortals. I promised them that one day, we would kill the lot of them. Once I brought Esmine back. Once the deed was done. As we'd done before, we would then flee for parts unknown. Lay low, as they say.

"Mr. Arnaud?"

"Yes, yes. Thank you, Mr. Thibault. What an honor to speak to such a lovely group of..."

I cast my spell over the crowd easily enough. As expected, they hung on my every word. I recited history I'd seen firsthand as I encouraged the gathering to believe in the supernatural. Yes, the paranormal had always been a part of this world and always would be. I hinted at some things, things I knew, but would never share my secrets entirely. More than once, I locked eyes with Patrice. It was strangely thrilling to see Esmine in such modern clothing. I hated modern attire. People cared nothing for mystery anymore but preferred to flaunt every perceived attribute. It did me no good to pine for ancient times. I needed Patrice to fulfill my deepest desire. To help Esmine return to me.

"Now, I will demonstrate to you here the power of the mind. A mind connected to the supernatural. Please, Patrice. Won't you join me?" I extended my hand to the shocked young woman. Her pretty eyes widened as she glanced around in an embarrassed fashion. "I need your help. Isn't she lovely?"

As the gathering offered polite applause, Patrice awkwardly left her clutch purse on the seat and came to my side. The darkened room seemed to glow a little brighter as she smiled up at me. Perhaps that was only my dull imagination. Wishful thinking.

I heard the hissing of my clan in my ears. It was a vampire's way of warning another vampire. I ignored their worries as I smiled toward their sparkling eyes. They continued to hang back, but they wouldn't be satisfied with hiding forever.

"As you can see, Patrice isn't wearing a wire." I spun her around as if we were dancing together. She laughed politely; it was a pretty sound. An all too familiar sound. She came to a slow stop, facing me with a nervous smile. "She has no idea what I am about to do. Do you, Patrice?" I kept my left arm around her waist.

"No, I don't. You're scaring me, Philip." She was telling the truth; I could tell by the timbre of her voice and the fast beating of her heart.

"No fear, dearest. No fear at all." My hand settled on the small of her back. "Trust me."

"Okay," she whispered back. I waved my right hand before her face slowly. Ah, yes. She was easy to work with. She relaxed slowly, and I repeated the move.

"Trust me, Patrice. Let your body relax. I will not let you fall," I purred in her ear. And she did just that. Her body sagged back, and her arms fell limp to her sides. I kept my hand on her back, but she'd surrendered her spirit. At least temporarily. I waved my hand again as the audience gasped. Patrice's legs began to rise. I waved my hand again, but this was merely showmanship on my part. Invisible hands were lifting her, following my command to the letter.

Patrice levitated higher and higher, and I removed my hand.

I smiled as the audience rose from their chairs and clapped excitedly. "Careful," I warned them playfully. "Don't wake her up just yet." I moved my hands, and the spirits obeyed me. They spun her around slowly and began to lower her again. As the hands delivered her to me, I put my arms around her.

With a soft kiss, she woke up. She started slightly but did not resist me. Her feet were firmly planted on the ground now, but my arms remained around her. With an elegant smile, I released her, spinning her once again in a mock dance.

"Curtsy, beautiful Patrice. You were marvelous."

The crowd flocked around us. Astounded, they were. Surprised and amazed. So many questions. So hungry for power. Except for Patrice. I kept her hand in mine. She did not pull away from the coldness of my skin. She did not pull away from me. She'd surrendered herself already, although she did not know it.

Lovely Patrice. You are mine now. You will be mine forever.

Chapter Four—Esmine

Sunlight beamed through the boudoir window of the Beauregard mansion. The stately home had become our family's escape and refuge, but it was not home. It could never be there. This was a wild place, despite this fine home and the bustling of the slaves, the willingness of local society to embrace us. No, never home. But France was in turmoil and not safe for people of pedigree any longer. The rumblings of revolution continued to shake our homeland. Surely history would not repeat itself. Surely not. Would the rabble rousers demand our heads as they had done with the former king and queen? Not that we were royalty, per se, but certainly we were an old and wealthy line. Heinous events occurred in my beloved France over fifty years ago, but the tension remained. The people of France were unhappy and looking for someone to blame for their poverty and disease.

Then, like Icarus, Philip descended, his wings wide and face bright from sailing close to the sun. He was our rescuer, winging us away from the danger that threatened us all. Strange that I would think of him so, knowing full well that Icarus did not have a good end. But Philip was not Icarus. He was handsome and elegant but not golden and shining. He was pale and thin, tall and strong. Philip rescued me from the prison of our circumstances. His intoxicating love and promises of a better life had captivated me and had captivated my Mama and Papa. I succumbed to his persistence in moving to this foreign land. My loneliness had taken the place of my fear and my sadness at leaving France behind. At least for now.

Yes, he had rescued me. Married me. Given me the safety he promised, but things were not right. My love for my husband remained, but the sad reality that he was not truly known to me introduced an unexpected sadness. Things had changed. I had changed, and I could not understand why.

"Madame," Louis said as he slowly opened the door. My butler carried a small silver tray, perfectly balanced on his white-gloved hands. On it was a piece of parchment tied with a blue ribbon. "A letter, Madame, from Monsieur Arnaud addressed from New Orleans."

Louis had been with my family for years. Mama and Papa insisted that Philip stay by my side, but he was frequently gone. In the beginning, he showered my parents with love and attention, but I was beginning to suspect that had been for my benefit. He did not truly love them, only wanted me. I was grateful for Louis' company in my loneliness.

More than anything, Philip longed for me to travel with him, but I was fearful at what we might find. I remained at the Beauregard Mansion with my parents while Philip pursued his adventures. Even now, he would not be thrilled about the idea of coming home but would do so graciously. And he never wavered in the appearance of his loyalty to our family. I was grateful for his commitment to duty.

"Merci, Louis." I nodded toward the marble-top table. "You can put it over there."

"Oui, Madame." He nodded slightly.

The three weeks that Philip had been gone had felt like three years.

"Louis," I called out after thinking for a moment.

"Oui, Madame?" he answered, setting the tray down as requested. His hands smoothed down his pressed black jacket. The strands of gray hair were slicked back away from his face, exposing his dark brown eyes. They were kind eyes filled with years of life.

"Do you know when this letter was sent?"

"No." His accent was still quite noticeable. Louis had no desire to speak English, but Philip required that he speak it while here in Savannah. New Orleans would be different, Philip insisted, because our culture would be embraced and dignified. And we would go to New Orleans, whether I liked it or not. Whether Mama and Papa liked it or not. Philip was our everything, our protector, our security. He was everything. I shivered at my own thought.

My gaze returned to the window. "Merci, Louis."

Our family is safe now, and that's all that matters. One day we can return, after the cries for revolution die down and the proper monarch is in place. None of us were safe there; the people did not want any royalty to keep their necks.

This was defiant thinking, against Philip's wishes, but at least my thoughts were my own. They still belonged to me. I held the parchment close to my lips and took in any remnants of Philip's scent before unfolding it. His words sprang from the page and filled my heart.

My dearest Esmine,

New Orleans has fulfilled all my expectations. It is a delightful city with joie de vivre that, I dare say, we would be hard pressed to find anywhere else. Opportunities and prosperity are abundant. The house I have found for us, it is as if it were built for us. Three stories tall with the finest of furnishings. You shall love it, my dear. Of that, I am sure. There is a wonderful view of the lake and many interesting ladies, all of whom long to make your acquaintance. You will not be alone anymore.

I shall return to Savannah within the week. Prepare the household. Tell your Mama and Papa that we will move within the month.

Forever yours, my darling,

Philip

I had many questions about his letter. What ladies was he referring to? Were these women his lovers? I suspected long ago that Philip had many, although I never had the courage to ask him about his life away from me. I did not want to think about this. I had other worries.

I stared out beyond the live oak trees that lined the lane to our home and sighed. I did not even have enough strength to pray again. In the letter, there was no mention of our baby, as I had hoped to read. No mention at all. How could he be so cold? Our child would be born soon, and then his heart would change. Once he saw the beauty of our child, he would love him or her.

"We will love you, petit," I whispered to my belly full of life. Philip had not been excited to have children. His response to my joyous announcement had been far from one of delight. I longed to have a family with him. Philip, however, wanted nothing to do with starting a family beyond the two of us. He would not celebrate the event, would not think about our growing family.

"Philip," I whispered, "come home to me and please love our child as you love me."

Clutching the life within me, I prayed for Philip's safe return. I prayed again that he would return home with a softened heart. Why did he run from our child? From his responsibility as a father? What was there to fear?

Two weeks later...

The pain of childbirth compared little to the anguish that consumed me as I looked at the beast that lay beside me. How could this be our child? How? I gagged again and threatened to vomit. Mama patted my back as she held the porcelain bowl. Philip stood within the shadows, peering at us. His lack of comfort shocked me. This was not the man that I had fallen in love with; he was the creator of this creature. He had done this to me. To my baby. Somehow, he had done it. Mama left with the hideous blob of flesh. She sobbed too.

I leaned back on the soggy pillows, unable to think what to say, until finally, I spat toward him, "Why didn't you tell me, Philip?"

"I tried, Esmine. You wouldn't listen," he hissed from the shadows again.

"You are a monster!" I screamed with rabid passion.

He moved closer to me as he shut the door. "You mustn't say those things. We will be together. You are all I need. We need no one else. I have spared your mother and father. I will spare them, but I will not let you go. I will make you one of us. We need nothing more than our love, Esmine. But we cannot have children. Never. It is not allowed. We are all the family that you would ever need."

"We?" I asked weakly. The loss of blood and the nausea threatened to pull me under. Take me back to the dark.

Philip looked around the empty room. "Yes, Esmine. Our kind."

"Our kind?" I repeated, staring down at the place where the gnarled, twisted body of the baby had rested. To think, I had nourished it with my body for months. "I don't...I don't understand, Philip. Our son, don't you care? Don't you care that my heart is broken?"

His dark eyes narrowed as he lunged toward me and covered me with heartless fury. "You are mine," he whispered viciously as he pierced my neck with his angry teeth. I could not speak for a moment as the warm liquid drained from me. "I will never let you go, my wife." Philip moved slowly away from me, and the dark red that covered his mouth contrasted with the glowing green in his eyes. How was that possible? Sometimes his eyes were warm and brown, others hazel, and now, they were unearthly.

Philip was unearthly. Unholy. Who was he?

My body began to reject the venom that he had gifted me. This was not love, nor was it the life that I desired. I grabbed the hand mirror from the nightstand to see firsthand if I was truly dying. "Mama!" I cried, but no words came. Not loud enough for her to hear me. The hand mirror revealed all. Evidence of his evil intention was left upon my neck.

"Don't worry, Esmine. You will not die—I will never let you die. You are mine forever. You will be happy, you'll see. We must drink blood, but leave it to me, my love. I will do the killing; I will do it all. Just to have you and keep you."

"This is not love, Philip. You would force me to live a life of eternal damnation? I will not do it!" I rejected his proposal while grabbing my neck. This bleeding must stop, or I would certainly perish. Maybe I should die? The agony of losing my child and discovering this horrible truth about Philip weighed on my mind and soul. Yes, I would welcome death. Truly, I would welcome it. But I could not let go of the hand mirror. I could not take my eyes off my reflection.

I glanced at my reflection once more and did not recognize it. Was I mad? My skin—it was gray and pale as if I were already dead, and my eyes were as dark as the night.

"You will not be like this for long," he assured me as he hovered in the shadows again. "Let the transformation happen. You must trust me. I too was unsure at first, but we belong together, my love. We have lived lifetimes before, and it is our destiny to live in this incarnation. You are mine, Esmine."

"No, I will not live this way. It is an abomination against God!"

"God?" Philip mocked me. "Wouldn't he want you to live forever?"

I searched the room for relief. An object, some weapon to use to end my misery. My eye fell on the low burning lamp. The only light in the dank, blood-soaked room. "May you forever die, Philip. I love you no more."

With all of my strength—and I had riled up more than I believed possible—I reached for the lamp and poured out the fiery kerosene onto my body. I heard myself screaming, but I did not fight against the pain.

Philip screamed. It was a wolfish, monstrous sound, but it relieved my mind. As I thought this, my soul began to separate from my tortured body. Yes, I was being released from my earthly prison.

Oh! I could see them around Philip. The Dark Ones. Pale and gesticulating, writhing and crying. Hanging on him, a bevy of demonic lovers. They reached for me too, and their eyes bled tears as Philip wailed again. They could reach all they wanted. I was beyond them now. Beyond them forever.

I was no longer among the living.

Chapter Five—Aggie

The coffee shop had its usual flow of customers mixed with a delicious blend of the aroma of coffee and baked goods. Hints of cinnamon and butter flowed around the entire shop, with the occasional scent of hazelnut tempting even the most die-hard French vanilla enthusiasts. Typical coffee shop. Heaven on earth.

"Why such a long face?" Phoenix asked me suspiciously. His handsome features darkened slightly. I had received another cryptic message from Patrice. Most of her texts were short and to the point lately. But this one...it had hints of something else. Was she seeing someone? If so, why wouldn't she tell me? We never kept secrets from one another. That wasn't something we did.

I'll be home late. Don't wait up. Love, Patrice.

"It's just Patrice. She's being all mysterious lately. I'm worried about her. She usually wants to talk about everything. I miss having my sister around," I confessed as I dumped more sugar into my already over-sweetened drink. Weird how I like the smell of coffee more than actually drinking it. I'm more of a tea person.

"I think you're being a little overprotective of your big sister. She's a grown woman, Aggie. She can take care of herself, and who knows? Maybe she's involved with someone." Phoenix winked at me and grinned. I refrained from doing what I really wanted to do at that moment. Slap the grin off of his face. He was annoyingly charming at times, and I was being serious. He was being Phoenix.

"I mean it, Phoenix. Something is up with her. She's been really sneaky lately. Avoiding my calls, staying out all night. Dressing like a hoochie-mama. She's not Perfect Miss Patrice anymore."

Phoenix blew on his coffee. "Hoochie-mama? I can't imagine that. Could be that she's seeing someone. Maybe someone you wouldn't approve of, or so she believes. You can be a little judgmental sometimes." He had us mixed up, obviously. I blew on my coffee and rolled my eyes.

"No way. Patrice was the goodie-two-shoes in high school, not me. I was the judgee, not the judger. Remember, I get along with everyone. I was the one that screwed up all the time. It was never the other way around. Besides, there's no way that she would keep that kind of secret."

"Aggie, all I'm saying is that maybe she just wants to do her own thing. You don't have to know every move she makes, do you?" His words were like a punch in the gut. Maybe he was right? Patrice was a grown woman.

"Fine, I'll keep my cool for now, but I'm telling you, my Spidey senses are tingling. I just can't put my finger on it yet, but there's a problem."

Phoenix leaned back. "Don't look for problems, Aggie. Let your sister do her thing. Come on, Spidey. Just give it some time. I'm sure Patrice will come around and let you know what's been going on when the time is right. She knows how much you've been through recently and how busy you are, and she probably wants to give you space. Speaking of your space, how's that art project going?"

After the hell we all had been through with the demon child, I had turned back to my art. I had to get images that perpetually infiltrated my dreams and nightmares out onto the canvas. It was therapeutic. Those poor lost souls that I couldn't help haunted me.

"It's going. I've only completed one painting so far in the series. Maybe I am too ambitious. I should focus on the painting and not commit to an entire series."

"That's probably a good idea." He flashed one of his enchanting grins at me. The kind that makes my heart melt every single time. I wanted so much more from him. More than what he could give.

"How about you and that new song of yours? Any progress?"

His gaze looked past me into the crowd. Nothing unusual for Phoenix. He had become more distant the more his abilities had come to the forefront. "No, I've written a few lines here and there. The music just seems to be harder to get to now..."

My hand found his. "I get it. Believe me."

He sighed as he squeezed my hand briefly and released it. I pretended that it didn't bother me. "Everything seems a little wonky these days, Ags. It's like everything around me seems out of focus. I try to sit down and write like I used to, but the words and melody just don't ring true to me anymore. It's hard to write a song about your life when you hardly recognize it. I've been trying to get a handle on it, though. It's getting a little easier. I think."

"Phoenix..." I moved my head slightly, bringing his gaze back to me. "I know it's been difficult. Trust me, I know. Nothing ever makes sense with the paranormal. I mean, it's even in the name. Para-normal."

He flashed that amazing smile. "You know, you annoy me with your sarcasm."

"Yes, and that's what I'm here for, to annoy the crap out of you. Don't let this take over your life. You are still you, just a little more in tune with your surroundings. I mean, use that to your advantage, Mr. Rock Star. What other songwriter out there can say that they speak to dead people?"

"You have a point," he replied with a chuckle. "Although I might have to come up with a catchy theme song now that I'm a paranormal investigator by day and a rock star by night. Maybe along the lines of *Ghostbusters*?"

I gave him a look. "Don't even go there. That song makes my skin crawl. Way too cheesy, even for you."

"Thanks, Ags," he said with a wink. "Not to change the subject, but about your sister...are you going to stop being such a worrywart, or what?"

"Or what," I huffed at him. "And we were having such a wonderful moment there. Nice attempt to change the subject."

"I'm sorry, but I really do think you should let it go. You know, like the *Frozen* song." Naturally, he began to sing it loudly in the coffee shop.

I cupped my hand over his beautiful mouth. "Please stop. That's even worse than the *Ghostbusters* music."

"Just trying to lighten the mood."

"I promise to ease up on Patrice and her secret life if you promise to write that song. I can't wait to hear it."

He pointed at his head and said, "It's all in here. Just got to write it down."

"You should probably let it go, too. Just face facts, Phoenix. You are unusual, and you'll never fit in. Like me. Word to the wise, though, you weren't fitting in to begin with."

Another laugh. I was on a roll.

There would be no way that I was going to let anything go with my sister. I had to find out what was going on with Patrice. Something was very wrong. I could feel it in my blood. I had a cold chill thinking about it. Even my parents were sending me messages asking about Miss Perfect. That wasn't like Patrice at all, to be so distant from all of us.

Not at all.

What or who was causing her to be so distant from me? What was she hiding? Why did I believe she was in trouble? Call it a sixth sense or maybe sisterly love. Yeah, she wasn't getting away from me and my nosiness.

"We've got some interesting things at the shop, Phoenix. Want to stop by and see them?"

"What did you guys get in?"

I sipped my coffee and offered a cryptic smile. "Oh, we have these tiny silver teacups, and they have engravings in the base of each cup."

"No more teacups, please."

It was my turn to laugh now. "Okay, then. We have a set of Victorian funeral photos. Totally cool. Totally creepy."

"Do tell."

"Well, thanks to high mortality rates and the rampant spread of disease, death was everywhere during the Victorian era. So, people came up with creative ways to remember the dead—including death photos. While it may sound gross today, families used postmortem photos to memorialize their lost loved ones. They are actually quite fascinating if you can get past the fact that they're dead people. Sometimes their eyes are open. They posed the bodies too. The babies are the saddest. We have a big book of them. Henri thinks he can sell it to a collector, but I'm not so sure."

"Really? I would buy that. I think it sounds fascinating. How much is he asking?"

"Okay, now I'm questioning everything about you. He hasn't made the price official yet. Are you going to eat that cookie?"

"No, you can have it. I'm seriously curious about that book, Aggie. I'm going to come by and take a look at it. Maybe tomorrow, if you're there."

"Yep, I'll be there. Come by anytime. I practically work nonstop since Patrice ducks out all the time."

"Ducks out? You mean she's not working her shifts?"

I sighed and clammed up. He didn't need to hear about our problems. I'd already told him too much. All I did was whine lately. "It's fine. Listen, I better split. I've got to go to the grocery store before I go home. See you tomorrow, okay?"

"Yep. It'll be after ten. I've got an appointment in the morning."

I didn't want to pry, so I didn't ask, although I was curious, naturally. I hugged him and was surprised when he gave me a quick peck on the lips. Surprised but happy.

I practically danced to the grocery store.

Chapter Six—Henri

I paced between the workroom and the store a few times before giving up. I'm not one to forget things, but I was plumb stymied. I know for a fact that I left that hairbrush and mirror set under a clean cloth on my workbench. I'd done a light polishing. Not enough to wipe away the patina. Buyers came to Devecheaux Antiques to find beautiful old things, things with character and history. This particular set was fairly new to the shop and, although selling the items would not pay for a weekend in New Orleans, they would certainly fetch a good price. But I didn't do this for the money. I felt a bit like a broker. These beautiful old things needed to find new homes with people who would love and appreciate them.

"Patrice?" I asked as I approached the counter. "I had some items on my workbench. A mirror and a brush. Have you put them out already? I don't see a listing on the computer."

Patrice lowered her eyes as she closed the drawer. "No, sir. I haven't seen those items lately. I haven't put them out. Maybe Aggie did. Need some help looking?" She finally smiled at me and met my eyes evenly. I was not a human lie detector like my wife, and I didn't want to believe anyone here had sticky fingers. No, that couldn't be it. I must be getting old. Too distracted.

"Sure. An extra pair of eyes would be helpful. Maybe I put them in storage by mistake. Are you sure you haven't seen them?"

Patrice smiled patiently as she tucked a strand of hair behind her slightly oversized ear. "There's so many things in here. I can see where it would be easy to lose something. I've done it before. You say you had them on the workbench?"

I murmured a yes, and we began our search. I was completely flabbergasted. Thirty minutes later, I was sweating. We heaved boxes in and out just in case I had actually placed the items in a storage box. No, this wasn't right. I know for a fact I left them on my bench.

"Are you sure you haven't seen them? I know I left them here. Is your sister home?"

"No, I mean...I have seen them, but I can't say when I last saw them. Um, I think Aggie is out, but I can go upstairs and check. Do you want me to pop up?"

"Please? I've got someone coming to look at the brush and mirror in about an hour. She's driving in from Pensacola."

"Okay." Patrice scurried out of the room, and I answered the doorbell. Someone had entered the shop, and I couldn't spend more time searching for lost items. I left my wife a voicemail, but she hadn't called me back yet.

Great, it was Mrs. McGregor. She was an hour early, and there was nothing I could do about it. "Hey there, Mrs. McGregor. Welcome back. How was your drive? I see you beat the rain."

We began an easy conversation, and thankfully she found a painting she fell in love with. Her words, not mine. I tried not to keep glancing at the door that led to the apartment, but so far, Patrice was a no-show. What was taking her so long? Something fishy was going on with her. I didn't want to believe anyone who worked for me would be a thief, but I was beginning to have some doubts.

Detra Ann breezed into the shop, and I couldn't help but feel relieved. As always, my wife was the most beautiful woman in the room, no matter where we went. But she was more than a trophy wife. Detra Ann Devecheaux was also the smartest woman I knew. Surely, she'd know what to do.

"Excuse me, Mrs. McGregor. I'll be right back."

"Okay," she said as she smiled through tea-stained teeth. Lovely lady. Bad teeth. I tried not to flinch. Still, I'd like to keep our well-traveled customers happy.

"Did you get my message?"

"What message? I was busy with our daughter. What's wrong? Where's Patrice?" She bombarded me with questions as she always did when she was trying to get to the bottom of something. In this case, a potential disaster.

"Mrs. McGregor is here to look at the mirror and brush set, but I can't find either piece. I know I left them on my bench. I asked Patrice about it. She hasn't seen them. I'm at a loss here. Have you seen them?"

Detra Ann hurried to the coatrack and deposited her raincoat. "Hmm...I saw you working on them. I know you left them there. The girls must know something. Where is Patrice?"

"Upstairs. She's been gone for fifteen minutes. I asked her to check with Aggie. Oh, shoot. Here comes Mrs. McGregor. How much longer can I stall her?"

"I'll keep her happy while you get to the bottom of it. Someone needs to come up with those pieces. Quick, fast, and in a hurry. Oh, shoot. How did I get juice on my skirt? Your daughter."

"Hey," I said as I pretended to be aggravated. Funny how Chloe was *my* daughter whenever she did something wrong. "You're gorgeous. Knock her out, tiger. I'll go find Patrice."

But there was no need to go in search of Patrice. She came through the small door that led upstairs, and the mirror and brush were in her hands. Her expression was blank, emotionless. Besides feeling angry, I also felt betrayed. How was it that we had searched the workshop for thirty minutes when they were upstairs the whole time? Unless Aggie took them without her knowing it.

To my surprise, Detra Ann hoofed it toward us. Her sassy bob bounced as she crossed her arms. "What's going on, Patrice?"

The petite young woman appeared startled by Detra Ann's arrival. Surprise, surprise. No one was afraid of me. My wife, that was another story. Not that she was mean. She was just a no-BS kind of gal. And did I mention she could spot a lie from a mile away?

"I don't know how these ended upstairs. I'm sorry. I can't explain it. They don't appear to be damaged."

"Why are you lying to us, Patrice? Does your sister know about this?"

"I'm not lying. I didn't mean to keep them." Oh, boy. That was denial but also a shift in her truth. So, she knew she had them all this time?

"You know I know. What is going on, Patrice?" I glanced over my shoulder at Mrs. McGregor, who was still quite intrigued with a collection of porcelain dolls on the other side of the store.

"I'm not sure what you mean. As I said, I don't know how they got up there. It must have slipped my mind when we were looking for them. Honestly. Sorry, y'all."

Detra Ann hadn't uncrossed her arms. She wasn't believing a word of it. Neither was I. "We'll talk about this later. Henri, finish your sale. I'll take these. Patrice, why don't you fix the front window? The book collection needs to be moved out of the sun."

Patrice handed the items over but didn't argue with her. Neither did I. "Sure. I'll take care of it."

I noticed she had her phone in her hand. Probably texting Aggie. Detra Ann and I glanced at one another. Her pretty lips were fixed in a firm line of disapproval. I knew what this meant. I agreed with her, but like she said, now was not the time.

"Mrs. McGregor, I am sorry about that. What else can I help you with today?" I didn't mention the mirror and brush, and neither did she. I thought that was odd, but I hoped she'd lost interest. I kind of wanted to hold on to them now. Especially if there was something paranormal going on. Of course there was. Why else would Patrice take them? Or Aggie? Was it possible that we had another haunted item? Luckily, Mrs. McGregor didn't mention the set she came for. Probably because she'd spent a small fortune on that doll collection and a trio of oil paintings.

Finally, the activity died down, and another customer blew through but blew back out again. The store was quiet, and I could feel the tension in the air. What now?

"What's going on with the mirror and brush, Patrice?" I decided to break the ice and get down to business. If possible, I wanted to leave Aggie out of this.

"I don't remember how they got upstairs, but I never meant to keep them. I was just using them." Patrice rose from the barstool behind the cash register. "You have to believe me."

"Why *don't* I believe you? Stop telling half-truths, Patrice. It's not like you to lie to us. None of this is like you. What is it about this set that has attracted you?" Detra Ann asked in an even, serious voice. I was proud of her for keeping her cool about everything.

"I need to use the mirror. Not forever, just for now. I'm sorry I didn't tell you. I'm really sorry to you both."

"What do you need it for? Use it how? It's just a mirror. Right?" I interjected, but the pit of my stomach twisted. Patrice shed a tear but didn't appear to be forthcoming with more information. Why was she being so reserved? "You have to let us know what's going on, Patrice. You work for us, and you live here. Why are you being so secretive?"

Before Patrice could answer, Aggie came in. Her bright, sunny smile quickly faded as she read the room. "What's everyone doing? Did I miss a meeting?"

"I have to go. Sorry, everyone." Before we could argue with her, Patrice grabbed her purse and was out the door. The doorbell chimed after her, leaving a deafening silence in her wake.

Chapter Seven—Patrice

The sound of my footsteps echoed throughout the apartment. To say I felt like a real heel would be an understatement. I refused to answer my phone, even though Aggie called me nonstop for at least an hour after my hasty departure from the shop.

I tried to stay as quiet as possible, but the old wooden floors were having none of that. They signaled my every move. Aggie was in the next room sleeping. I wanted to keep it that way. She knew I had been avoiding her, and a game of ten thousand questions was the last thing I wanted to play. The Devecheauxs were right to think I had not been completely honest lately, but secrecy was required for what I had to do. I was going to return the items eventually. But now Detra Ann had the mirror and brush. Maybe I could get them back...

It's not like Aggie had never borrowed anything from the shop. Why was it such a big deal when I did it?

I sat in the quiet of the apartment and my cheeks flushed as I remembered the night I'd just had with Philip, his lips pressing against mine and our bodies moving together. It had never been like this with anyone else. Never. When I was with Philip, time seemed to stand still. He made me weak, powerless. I happily surrendered to his touch every time. My breath quickened just thinking about it.

"Nice seeing you here." Aggie's voice cut through my memory like a sharp knife cutting butter.

"Aggie! Thanks for giving me a heart attack." I clutched my chest as I sat on my bed. I'd barely got my bearings before she broke into my room.

"Why are you sneaking around, Patrice? And what's up with this get-up? You look like you're going to a funeral. Are you in trouble? Tell me the truth."

I snorted at her assumptions. "Why would you assume I am in trouble? I do live here, you know. I'm not sure what you mean by new attire..."

"You wouldn't know it from my end. That circle of hickeys on your neck is pretty damn telling," Aggie bitterly popped back. "You're never here, and when you are here, you hide out in your room. And by new attire, I mean all these dark clothes. It's like you've gone goth or something."

Aggie flopped down in the oversized chair and folded her arms. Her disapproving glare made my body stiffen. This was the moment I had dreaded.

"I'm the big sister, remember? I know you don't think I'm supposed to have a life, Aggie, but I do. And believe it or not, you don't have to be the center of it."

"Really? What are you hiding from me?" Aggie's voice cracked. Clearly, she was hurt by my separation. "You must be doing some pretty shady stuff lately. Not a very good role model for your little sister. What's happening to you? You used to be so full of life, and now it's like you're the grand dame of the walking dead."

I ignored her damp eyes and the concern I heard in her voice. "It's none of your business, Aggie, but if you must know, I met someone. There is nothing shady going on; I finally found someone I can confide in. He loves me and wants to spend time with me. You have Phoenix and the Devecheauxs, and now I have Philip."

Aggie bit her bottom lip. "Who's Philip? Why can't I meet him?"

"Why would you? Philip Arnaud is his name. I met him at a conference. We hit it off. He's a really interesting guy."

"What kind of conference?"

"A paranormal conference, if you must know. I went there to find out more information about what I was going through, what you were going through. I didn't want to cause you any more concern. You've had your hands full recently, and I just..."

Aggie's demeanor changed quickly. "You didn't want to bother me. That's rich."

"Yes, it's true," I replied defensively. "You'll like Philip. I did intend to introduce you two."

"Highly unlikely that I will like him," Aggie fired back. "I don't like the fact that this stranger knows about us. Me and you. What if he tells other people? Mom and Dad still don't know about us."

Throwing my hands up, I exclaimed, "You're not even going to give Philip a chance? That's really mature, Agnes. He's not a stranger. He's my boyfriend." Okay, that might not be accurate, but I was in the heat of the moment now. "We are seeing each other, and I haven't told him *anything* about you. I know you probably find that hard to believe. You seem to think you're the center of the universe."

"Center of the universe? How dare you say that to me! I am your sister! I got this job, and I found this apartment. Philip

Arnaud can't be on the up and up if you can't bring him around the people who love you. I don't see why you're rushing into things with this Philip guy. You could have any guy in town. Don't you think it's a bit odd that this man shows up and now your whole life revolves around him?"

My face grew hot with anger, and my hands balled up into fists. I fought the urge to hit her. "Why are you jealous of us? You've always been jealous of me. I thought that since you finally had someone in your life, this behavior would stop. I guess you'll always be stuck in my shadow, Aggie. Always trying to be me!"

I hadn't physically punched her, but my words had hit her deeper than any fist would have. I instantly regretted saying them.

She met my glare with one of her own. She was on her feet now. Would this come to blows? "I'm not jealous of you, Patrice! Not anymore. If you can't see that I'm trying to protect you, then I guess we have nothing more to say here. But you need to make it right with Henri and Detra Ann if you're not going to keep up your end of the bargain with your job. They trust me, and I can't lose that."

I reached out to her, grabbing her hands in mine. "Aggie, I'm sorry. I didn't mean that."

"Yes, you did. You meant every word of it, Patrice. Go do your thing. I hope you're happy."

The tension between us was palpable, but cutting through it would have to wait. One day, she would understand how I felt. I loved Philip more than anything in this world.

Nothing, not even Aggie, would stand between us. But she was right that I would have to talk to Detra Ann and Henri.

They knew about the brush and mirror, even if Aggie didn't. They deserved an explanation, and I hoped I could come up with one that would suffice.

Chapter Eight—Aggie

"Our journey is coming to an end," the monotone voice said, startling me out of a deep sleep.

Sleep didn't come as easily as it used to. My mind raced, and then the nightmares came. Dark dreams that were not easily shaken. I hated this horrible rut of sleeping patterns I'd fallen into.

"You got that right," I announced to the darkness, pulling the earphones out of my ears. I pulled my legs up and dangled them off the side of the bed. "Our journey has come to an end because you scared the crap out of me." I didn't put much thought toward my bad dreams, but I was so tired. So very tired.

I had tried for weeks to lull myself to sleep with guided sleep meditations. The white noise helped at first, but not lately. That heated conversation with Patrice kept replaying in my head like a broken record. Why had I said that? Why had she said that? What was happening to us? What should I do? Call my parents? Call the police? Call someone?

Finding a comfortable spot on my bed was impossible these days. Every muscle in my body found every lump in the mattress. Nothing I did gave me any sense of comfort, physically or mentally. Everything felt wrong and out of place.

Who was this Philip? I was going to have a chat with this dude.

The urge to go and plunder through my sister's room was too strong to ignore. There had to be some sort of evidence or sign of where Patrice had been spending her time. Maybe something that might tell me where that black ribbon had come from. Of course, with all the black she was wearing now, it made more sense that she'd have it.

I tiptoed down the hallway, stopping only to make sure that she wasn't home. *Of course she wasn't.* No one was there but me, my thoughts and my loneliness.

Maybe this was all in my head and Phoenix was right? May as well plunder away.

Looking around Patrice's room, a wave of guilt lodged in my throat. I had turned into our nosy mother, who always snooped around our rooms for evidence of wrongdoing. I guess it's true—you do turn into your parents. I shook that thought out of my mind. This was to help Patrice, not hurt her. We weren't teenagers anymore, and I had to know what was going on with her. What if she brought some weirdo back to our apartment?

Hmm...

Nothing seemed out of place. Every book on her bookshelf was neatly and alphabetically organized. Her makeup was arranged on the vanity. I opened the closet doors to find every article of clothing color-coordinated, as usual. Light to dark, shirts to blouses, jeans to pants. Patrice had always been more organized than the average bear. Or me.

Nothing unusual here. I plopped down on the bed, remembering the few times I had confided in Patrice in this very room. We talked about guys and my angst against her old cheerleading friends. She listened even though I knew she had no idea how I was truly feeling. How could she? We had grown much closer since high school. Or at least I thought we had. Her bed was comfortable and soft and smelled like her perfume. I ran my hand under the pillow and was met by something unexpected.

"What the hell?" I exclaimed to no one, pulling out the object.

A dark velvet bag.

I pulled the drawstring on the bag and dumped out the contents. The smooth garnet stone caught the light coming from the inside of Patrice's closet, causing a light red reflection to bounce off the walls. It was mesmerizing. I tried not to touch it.

"This looks expensive," I muttered out loud. "Whoever owned this had big bucks." Where did it come from? Had it come into the shop? If so, why was it up here?

Why is Patrice stealing stuff from the shop? Why would she do this?

I moved closer to the ring, trying to examine the inner markings, but I couldn't make them out. "Tell me your secrets," I whispered, slipping the ring onto my index finger.

Candlelight flickered against the plaster walls. The warmth of the air filled the space, along with the smell of jasmine. I looked around the room, trying to make out my surroundings.

The room I found myself in was spacious, with a four-poster bed and a rosewood sofa, wide-planked floors and floor-to-ceiling windows that let in the pale moonlight. I felt my breath quicken as I took it all in.

Where was I? In my hand, I held a mirror. Now, this I had seen in the shop! I slowly turned it around.

My hands began to shake as a strange reflection was revealed.

The face that stared back at me could have been Patrice with dark hair. Beautiful and radiant. Full, plump rosy lips and cheeks. Eyes that sparkled and hair that framed her face perfectly. She could have been a painting.

Who was she?

"Darling," a voice cut through the darkness. "You must be tired, my dear."

The shadowy figure moved closer. It glided across the floor. The presence—his presence—consumed the room. He blocked out the moonlight. I tried to make out his features, but they were blurred. Nothing would come into focus. Nothing except his piercing, ever-changing eyes. Dark and green and then something else.

"I can't see you," I replied.

His hands protruded from the darkness, revealing the garnet ring. "You don't need to see me."

The ring! Who are you?

I turned the mirror around once more to view the reflection. The face that had been beautiful and radiant was now drawn and pale. Her eyes were sunken and dark. The once-ruby-red lips, drained of all color, repeatedly mouthed a word. A word that brought me out of the vision shaking.

My clothes clung to me. Sitting straight up in the middle of Patrice's bed, I called out the name that flowed from the past.

"Esmine!"

Oh, no! Patrice was caught up in something much darker than I *ever* expected. I headed straight to Phoenix's house—I needed his help. Now.

"Calm down," Phoenix said as he wrapped his hands around my shoulders. "Tell me everything that happened."

My voice shook. "I found something in Patrice's room and went into a vision. I saw other things there, things from the shop!"

"I told you not to go snooping," Phoenix shot back, "and you know how I feel about you going into one of your visions alone. It's not safe, Aggie."

I refused to get lured into a fight about something this unimportant. "I know, Phoenix. But I had to do something about Patrice, and it's a good thing I didn't listen to you. My sister is caught up with evil. I mean—he's pure evil. Philip Arnaud is evil!"

He put his wide hands up to calm me down. "Wait a minute! What did you see in the vision? Tell me everything."

"I saw enough. More than enough." Esmine's face flashed in my memory. "In the vision, I had the mirror from the shop in my hands. And when I turned the mirror over, there was a reflection. I saw a woman."

"That's not strange. I mean, you normally do see a reflection in mirrors." Phoenix scoffed with disbelief. "You saw yourself? Are you sure you weren't dreaming?"

"No. I think I know my own reflection. Not someone else's. The other thing is, the reflection I saw could have been Patrice. The woman looked exactly like her; the only difference was the hair color—and the clothing. I swear it could have been her twin. Twins that lived a few hundred years apart."

Phoenix's face drained of all its color. "Was it really Patrice?"

"No, it wasn't Patrice. I mean, I'm pretty sure it wasn't. He wants it to be, though. Philip wants my sister to become Esmine!"

"Let's take a step back. Normally, your visions connect you to people that are haunting the object, right?"

"Yes, that's normally the case," I agreed as I held his hand.

"Well, we know that Patrice isn't haunting the object, so it has to be someone different. Someone from the past that is connected to it. This Esmine is trying to warn you, I think." Phoenix brushed his hair back away from his forehead. "Who could it be if it's not Patrice?"

"Doppelganger?" I joked, trying to cut the tension.

"Not funny," he said with a frown. "Those things terrify me."

My hands tensed up in defense. "You're right. I'm just a little freaked out right now. There's something else I need to tell you."

"What?" Phoenix's eyes narrowed. "What else?"

I let out a breath. "The object that I found in Patrice's room was a ring; it's the same ring that I saw in the vision. All the objects, the mirror, brush, and ring, are connected. The man in my vision was wearing the ring. He's got something to do with the lady and the mirror. I'm not sure right now how they are all connected, but they are definitely connected."

He paced the floor. "Patrice was drawn to the ring enough to steal it from the shop. And maybe the other items too. Why? That's not like your sister."

"That's another question I can't answer. No, it's not like Patrice to steal anything. She's always been Miss Goodie-Two-Shoes. The only thing that has changed in her life is this new guy. I don't trust him."

Phoenix stopped. "I hate to admit it, but I think your sister is in some trouble here. You were right, Ags."

"Thank you for that. Now will you help me?" I asked, kind of exasperated.

"I think I may know someone who can help us. He's in a covert, underground group, but I think that's what we need at the moment. Of course, he's probably going to need a little more information than just a reflection in a mirror that looks like your sister."

"Like what? What kind of information. Who do you know that belongs to a covert, underground group? Phoenix, you're a man of mystery."

He kissed my cheek. "Unfortunately, you need to go back into the vision and find out some more info. You've got to ask this Esmine person who the man is and what he wants. Is it really Philip? Someone else?"

I shrugged. "That won't be difficult. There were markings on the inside of the ring, but I couldn't make them out. After what I saw, I didn't want to touch the dang thing again. It was just...too much, but I think I can do it now. If you are with me."

Phoenix flashed his beautiful, comforting smile. "Of course. I wouldn't want you to be alone."

"I appreciate that." I returned the smile.

He shifted in his seat as his smile faded. "I'm also afraid that you're going to have to tell Detra Ann and Henri. They really need to know what's going on."

"I agree. They need to know. I just don't know what to say."

"Tell them the truth. That's all you have to do."

Phoenix *was* right. I grabbed my phone to send off a text. It was late, and I knew that a conversation would just have to wait until the morning. Detra Ann would be at the shop soon enough, and the text would have to do for now.

"Can I spend the night here? I don't want to go back to my apartment tonight. If Patrice shows up and sees that I've taken the ring..." I paused. "Well, I don't know what she will do or how she will act." The warmth of his hand on my lower back relaxed me. It was reassuring, and I welcomed the gesture.

"Of course." His lips brushed my forehead as I melted into his arms. "I'm always glad to have you."

"Have me? What do you mean?"

With a sudden seriousness on his face, he said, "Aggie, I'm here for you. You know that, right? No matter what."

"Yes. I know."

"Good. Just making sure." For a moment, everything melted away. The ring and Patrice. Everything.

It was just Phoenix and me in each other's arms. No, nothing else mattered for the rest of the night. We escaped our worries, all our fears, and dove into our passion.

Into each other.

The whole world disappeared.

Chapter Nine—Patrice

My heart fluttered as I headed to my appointment with Philip. I put the address that he'd given me into my GPS. It was an unfamiliar area to me, and my inner compass was lacking. I preferred to navigate by landmarks.

The mansion was on the outskirts of town. Philip found it through a rental-by-owner website and had promised it would be the perfect romantic getaway for us. He would be leaving soon, and he wanted me to go with him. I didn't even know where we were headed. What was going on with this whirlwind romance? My thoughts went to Aggie and her unwarranted disdain for Philip. How could she not like him when she hadn't even met him yet? If she would only give him a chance.... Well, to be fair, I'd kept him a secret. I had kept him all to myself.

A dark, narrow road led me through the woods. Winding and twisting, the gravel road crunched under my tires. I hadn't ventured this far outside of the city limits since I was in high school. Like many of my classmates, I went looking for ghosts and believed in the legends of headless spirits that chased people down Cricket Lane.

Hmm... This was the perfect setting for someone studying the occult. Spooky and dark.

Checking myself in the mirror, I couldn't help but smile at the thought of us finally being alone. I glanced at the black velvet bag that held part of my guilt. The reflection that had stared back at me that night had haunted me ever since. What would the Devecheauxs say when they realized I'd stolen the set a second time?

The car jolted a little, bringing me back to reality. What in the world? It felt like I had hit a pothole or a small animal.

Thump. Thump. Thump.

I pulled off onto the side of the narrow road, onto what little shoulder there was to move to. Only my headlights illuminated the road in front of me. No other cars were in sight.

My cell phone's battery light was red. I picked it up to text Philip. The wheel of battery death began to spin. How had I overlooked this?

"No, no, no!" I screeched at the dying phone until the last bit of life evaporated from it. "Great, Patrice. Now what?" I muttered, throwing the phone back on the seat.

Headlights hit my rearview mirror.

A dark figure moved closer to my car; I couldn't make out any features at first. I watched in the side mirror as the person moved closer.

Tap. Tap. Tap.

Rolling my window down just a few inches, I looked up at the man who now stood right outside my door. "You need help?" a friendly voice asked. He didn't look like a serial killer.

"Yes," I responded through the small crack at the top of my window. "I believe it's my tire."

"I'll check it out." The man returned quickly. "You're right, ma'am. The tire on your passenger's side is pretty messed up."

I rolled my window down a little further. The man's features became clearer. Strong jaw, kind, crystal blue eyes. Yeah, just the type of person that could be a serial killer.

He reached out his perfectly manicured hand. "I'm Mark."

"I'm Patrice," I said as I shook his hand gingerly.

"Nice to meet you," he replied with a smile. "You got a spare?"

"I think so, in the back."

Mark looked at me for a moment. "Can you open the door, or do you need help?"

I shook my head. "No, I'm sorry. It's just that..."

"I'm not a weirdo or anything."

"Well, that's what a weirdo would say."

He backed away from the car with his hands up. "You've got a point. Look, I'll stand over here while you get the spare, and then you can hop back in the car if you want."

"Thanks."

"Not a problem."

I slowly opened the door, keeping my eyes glued on this tall, dark and handsome stranger that just appeared out of nowhere. This felt weird. I needed normalcy. "Where are you from?"

"Originally?"

"Yes, originally," I said as I opened the hatch and retrieved the spare tire.

"I'm from Citronelle originally, but I've been living in New Orleans and Savannah."

Rolling the spare to him and keeping my keys tightly squeezed between my fingers, I asked, "New Orleans and Savannah? What do you do?"

Mark grabbed the spare and went to work changing the shredded tire. "Construction, mostly. A few side gigs here and there."

"What kind of side gigs?" I asked, intrigued.

Never taking his eyes off the task at hand, he said, "I enjoy building things and investigating different types of architecture and historical places. I decided to settle between the two cities because their histories fascinate me. Some interesting characters have found their way to both places."

"Mobile has fascinating people and architecture too. Why not live here?"

He paused. "Good question. I guess I just never felt the urge to live in Mobile. Maybe because I wanted to get as far away from my roots as possible while I was young and had the energy to do it." Mark tightened the last bolt and stood up. Wiping the dust off of his faded jeans, he continued, "You're right, though. Mobile does have some fascinating characters."

"Maybe you should rethink your desire to flee from your roots?" I smirked.

His hand smoothed down his thick brown hair as he looked down at the ground. "I'll take that into consideration. Looks like you're all set, Miss Patrice."

I returned the smile. "Thank you."

"Not a problem. Lucky thing I took this shortcut," he said with a wink. "You might have been out here all night. No telling what kind of monsters lurk out here in these woods."

I shut the car door behind me and rolled the window down all the way. "Good thing. Thanks again," I replied, waving out the window.

But he was gone. What the hell? Where did he go? Okay, my eyes were playing tricks on me. Surely, he was just on the other side of the road... I got out of the car and looked but saw nothing. What was going on? I took another look but decided to leave. Philip was waiting. He was all that mattered.

Chapter Ten—Aggie

Devecheaux Antiques was lit up by a few of the antique lamps that were some of Detra Ann's favorites. Highly ornate and in good working condition, they showered the shop in warm yellow light. They were beautiful Tiffany lamps. Delicate and beautiful, like the Boss Lady herself. I switched them off and turned on the overhead lights as I always did when I opened the shop. I joined the rest of the party in the workroom. We weren't open to the public yet, and there was a good reason for that.

"What's going on, Aggie?" Henri sat across from me. "When we got your text late last night that just said you really needed to talk to us this morning, we got a little concerned."

"I'm sorry about that, but I wanted to make sure that you both got here as soon as possible this morning. If it wasn't time-sensitive—if it wasn't serious, I wouldn't have been so desperate. Patrice doesn't know what she's doing, y'all. She doesn't know at all. She thinks she's in love, but he's trouble. Bad trouble."

"Spit it out, Aggie," Detra Ann chimed in. "You are starting to scare me. Is this about the items from the Beauregard Mansion?"

"Yes, but I'm positive it's not about stealing."

"We noticed on the inventory sheet that she hadn't marked the antique mirror and brush set down, and we looked everywhere in the shop." Detra Ann handed me the list. Sure enough, everything was marked but the antique mirror and brush set. "She brought them down from your apartment and told us she couldn't remember how they had gotten up there. I took them from her that day, and now they're missing again. If she can't give us a good reason why, we're going to have to let her go. I hate to do it, but we can't allow this to continue."

I dumped the items out of the bag onto the counter. "I don't know where she might be keeping the mirror and brush, but I found this ring under her pillow."

Detra Ann reached for the ring. "This is from the Beauregard Mansion collection? I don't even remember seeing this piece."

"Why would she lie to us?" Henri asked me. He was clearly hurt.

"We don't know," Phoenix answered. "Tell them what you saw, Ags."

"May I hold it, Detra Ann?" She dropped it in my gloved hands. "I've had a feeling something wasn't right with Patrice for the last couple of months. She's never home, always stays out late, and has been hanging out with some questionable characters. We had a fight a few weeks ago, and she told me she's been seeing someone. I don't know anything about him except his name and that they met at some paranormal conference, but her whole personality has changed. And not for the better. The perky, happy-go-lucky cheerleader has been replaced by someone detached and absent from reality."

"What does that have to do with the mirror and brush and this ring?" Detra Ann interrupted.

"Last night, after I found this in her room, I had a vision. In my vision, I had the mirror from the shop in my hands. And in it, saw a woman that looked like Patrice's twin. I only got a name, but I think there's more to it. I think Patrice has become obsessed with this mirror, especially if she took it again, but I'm not entirely sure why."

"What do we need to do?" Henri asked. "Do you think the mirror is haunted, or is it Patrice?"

"Both, maybe. I'm not sure. With your permission, I'd like to hold on to the ring until I get the full story. I want to experience another vision with it."

Detra Ann frowned. "Aggie, you know how I feel about all this. You need to be careful. We've been lucky so far, but sometimes that luck runs out. I have seen that happen firsthand. I'll never forget when Carrie Jo's mom passed away."

She knew all too well how all this could go south. I knew Detra Ann was worried, but I had no other choice. "I'll be careful."

Detra Ann caught Phoenix's eye. "You stay with her, but I can't be here. We've got to get home to Chloe. She's still not quite ready to be away from Mommy and Daddy for a long time. I can't take any chances."

Henri didn't look so sure. "Detra Ann, I think I should stay. One of us should stay."

Detra Ann's face crumpled, and I immediately felt terrible for her. I had to interject on her behalf. "It's fine, Henri. You need to be with your family. Phoenix and I can handle this. I promise it will be fine, but I have to help Patrice, whether she wants it or not."

Phoenix put his hand on mine. "I'll stay with her."

Henri rose and took Detra Ann's hand. At least he didn't argue about it. "Call us and let us know what you find out. We'll help any way we can." The door shut behind them, the bell tinkled, and I slowly removed my only protection between me and the other world. Time for the gloves to come off.

The darkness of the room faded away and the two figures became clearer. A dark-haired lady and the dark, shadowy figure from before. "Esmine, my love." The shadow moved along the walls of the old mansion. "Why do you deny me?" Was he real? A figment of Esmine's imagination? A ghost?

"I've not denied you," Esmine whispered, her voice trembling. "But I cannot do what you ask. I cannot do it. Our child—I gave birth to a monster!"

"We have no need of offspring, my love," the voice hissed from the darkness. "I created you to be with me forever, Esmine, and yet you have denied your eternal life with me."

I tried to focus on Esmine, my eyes squinting to see through the darkness. Finally, her face became clear. *Oh, God! She's dying!* Her dress was covered in blood, and there were two small entry wounds visible on her neck. "I will not become what you desire," she sobbed pitifully. "My baby! What have I done? What did you do to me? To our child?"

"What I desire is you for all eternity. How can you be so cruel? I have risked everything to be with you forever. You gave yourself to me, Esmine."

She moaned with pain and desire.

"Look at what you have done to me!" Esmine screamed, stepping toward the shadow. "This is not the life I wanted. Damned for all eternity. Doomed to be a killer, to live under a curse. I know what you are, Philip!" Her voice was weak, and she was clearly dying.

Philip! Is this Patrice's Philip?

Suddenly, the vision muted. They spoke, but I could hear none of it. I desperately wanted to. Would I lose my grip on the past? I clutched the ring tighter and stilled my breathing. Soon, I was back.

"Damned?" Philip growled from the darkness. "We are all damned. This world is a cruel place. At least with our eternal lives, we can be together. Forever! Together, we will enjoy the relentless pursuit of knowledge. It's what you always wanted, Esmine. Find the root cause of fear and destroy it. Yes, there is darkness in the world, but how can you fight dark with light? Only darkness can conquer darkness."

"You are mad! Only light can conquer darkness. Evil is evil, Philip!"

"I may be mad, Esmine, but you are wrong. We can conquer this together for eternity." A pale hand reached out from the darkness. "Join me. Join us. There are many others like me. You'll see."

"Never! I choose death!" With all of her strength—all of her agony and despair—Esmine reached up for the lamp and poured out the fiery kerosene onto her body. She screamed but did not attempt to save herself.

She screamed again, "I will never become what you are!" Philip screamed like the monster he was, and I couldn't help but scream myself.

"Get away from her!" I screamed, hoping to save her. I'd gone too deep. I'd gone too far. I could feel the heat, smell the burning flesh. Feel her agony. I began to cry. Then I felt a hand on me. A comforting, familiar hand. Phoenix!

I was back at the shop, away from Esmine.

What had she become? I knew, but I didn't believe it. I knew what they were, what she'd become!

Phoenix shook me. "Aggie, wake up!"

"I know what happened. I know what Philip is and what he's going to do to Patrice."

Phoenix hugged me and then put his hands on the sides of my face. "Are you alright? What did you see, Aggie? What is he?"

My whole body trembled at the memory. "A vampire. He's a vampire!" I collapsed into his arms. "He's on a mission to make my sister one of them. Philip wants to turn her. We've got to save her."

"I promise my friend can help us," he assured me. "You've got to trust me on this, Ags. This is beyond our expertise. But Mark will know what to do. He's our only hope."

"Call him, Phoenix. Please call him," I sobbed. "I'll do whatever it takes." I cried, "I can't lose my sister." I couldn't shake the sense of urgency I felt. The memory of Esmine's sunken, hopeless eyes.

It was now or never.

Chapter Eleven—Mark

If I had any doubts that I was destined to be here in Mobile, Alabama, at least for a little while, I didn't after that phone call. Philip Arnaud had been on my radar for a long time. A very long time. Fifteen years, as of last month. He was a dangerous man—no, make that creature—but also a careful one. Usually. But things were changing with him. I sensed Philip's tension, his evil focus. Sometimes I knew things about him, things I should not know because of the exchange.

I preferred to call it an exchange rather than what it was, an attack. He throttled me in a New Orleans alley, sliced my throat with his fingernail and drank my blood. But only briefly. Luckily for me, one of his bats, a lady in black, found him and persuaded him to spare me. I can't say why. I didn't know her, never met her. I couldn't even make eye contact with her. Their eyes glittered when they were hungry and, as I would discover later when I met her again, when they were feeling amorous.

I blushed at the strange experience and pushed it out of my mind. I knew her name now.

Juliette. Juliette.

I had to be careful not to think of her too much. I didn't want to call her to me in case she finished the job. I can't say why she was curious about me, why she liked me, but I didn't trust a vampire. None of them, and there were far too many vampires on this planet.

Yes, I already knew about this band of traveling vampires. I'd never met a more well-traveled group. The Brotherhood, of which I am a part, were committed to tracking paranormal creatures, haunted locations and psychic people. Someone needed to keep an eye on their movements, and for some reason, many of these old ones preferred the Gulf Coast. Strange, but true. This case, however, was most disturbing. Phoenix's suspicions were correct. The lovely Patrice was certainly in danger. I'd already met her on that back road near Cricket Lane. Yes, she was both lovely and naïve. That's what I picked up from her. I don't really have consistent psychic abilities, but I am pretty good at reading people. She was too young and inexperienced for an ancient creature like Philip Arnaud. And if my hunch was correct, she was the spitting image of Esmine de la Fontaine.

Did that mean what I thought it meant? I'd already placed a call to Nathan, my mentor. He was very interested in the crumbling Beauregard Mansion, and all the hair-raising history, including the complete slaughter of the Beauregard family, even their slaves. It was one of those horrible histories that nobody wanted to talk about. I seriously doubted whether the local residents even knew about it. It had been carefully quieted down over the centuries. Left out of the history books. Only spoken about in the shadows, or in the halls of the Brotherhood.

"Phoenix? Good to see you. How's the music coming?" I didn't wait for him to answer. "You must be Aggie. So nice to meet you. Phoenix tells me you are a psychometrist. I find that fascinating. Am I right that Patrice is your sister?"

Phoenix shook my hand, and I slid into the booth. This was a cozy diner, familiar even with the sticky seats and wobbly table. Were all diners alike? This place, called *Time To Eat*, had a kitschy clock theme. I hoped the food was good. It was always hit or miss with places like this. I was in the mood for pie and coffee and not much else. I stayed away from meat during investigations like this. I don't really know what Nathan expected me to do, except watch and observe. But now a friend was asking for my help. I couldn't just watch and observe.

"Aggie and I are happy that you agreed to meet with us. You're a difficult guy to get in touch with these days, Mark. The Brotherhood must be keeping you busy. Have you been traveling much?"

Aggie refused to follow the chitchat rules. There was no room for polite conversation with her today. I couldn't blame her, really. Her sister was in serious trouble, and Aggie was ready to get down to business. "You've met Patrice? How do you know Philip? What exactly do you know about him?"

"Patrice had a flat tire. I helped her change it. That was that. She was then on her way to Cricket Lane and there was no dissuading her. She was on her way to be with him, under the spell of the sparkling and devilish Philip Arnaud. He has laid claim to her, Aggie. He will turn her. I think that is his plan. I won't lie to you; it may be too late."

"I'm not going to just let her go, Mark. She is my sister. If I can reason with her, if you help us, we can get her out of the county, away from this man."

"And then what? Don't you know who she is?"

You could hear a pin drop with my last question. About this time, an overweight waitress shuffled toward us to take our order. I decided against the pie and just ordered coffee. Phoenix and Aggie asked for water. The waitress grunted impolitely and wobbled off to fetch our beverages. I was surprised that she didn't ask us to leave or at least demand that we order food.

"Yes, as I said, she is my sister. My big sister. She's always taken care of me, and now it's my turn to take care of her. And I've seen another woman. One that looks like Patrice. She killed herself because she didn't want to become a monster like Philip. And now Philip is back and thinks Patrice is Esmine."

"Patrice *was* Esmine, long, long ago, but they don't share a soul. Only their appearance. What Philip wants to do is far more sinister than merely killing your sister. He wants to summon Esmine's soul, through the use of a power object. He will take Patrice's life, or at least weaken her to the point of death so he can compel her to comply. Then he will force Esmine to return to him, force her to take up residence in Patrice's empty body."

"God!" Aggie gasped, and then I realized I'd been too heartless in conveying the analysis.

"Mark! Have a little tact," Phoenix scolded me as he put his arm around his girlfriend.

I wonder if he knows she will be the death of him...

And where did that come from? I glanced over toward the parking lot, hoping the thought wasn't my own. I picked up things from time to time, tiny prophecies, but they weren't usually that dire. No, this seemed to come from somewhere else. Was Philip watching us? Doubtful. He was too busy seducing Patrice. Of that, I was pretty sure. They were lovers, surely. At least that. If he hadn't already tapped into her blood supply.

Tiny nibbles. Only tiny nibbles.

And then I heard laughter in my mind. Oh, damn. Philip Arnaud knew we were here. He knew we were coming for him. I pulled my jacket collar up, as if that would protect me.

"Mark? What is it?"

I removed my phone from my pocket. "I am sorry if I hurt you, Aggie. I am sorry to be so blunt. It's not like me, I promise. I have been following Phil—I mean, the vampire for so long, I tend to think of anything that has to do with him in dark tones."

"But that's your opinion. He wants to kill Patrice. How do we stop him?"

"I'm not sure yet, but let's start with information. I will give you all the information I can. With your abilities—I sense both of you are strong in your individual talents—there is a possibility that we can reach her. But we need to move quickly. The Beauregard Mansion is derelict, barely standing, but he is there. For sure. He was here a few moments ago. He knows we are coming for him."

"Does he really? What do we do?" Phoenix sounded shocked. The waitress returned and again asked us to order. I succumbed to the pressure and ordered a basket of french fries. She returned with them rather quickly. None of us ate a one.

"This is a painting of the man himself." I handed my phone to the two young people. "It's a picture of an oil painting, commissioned nearly one hundred and sixty years ago. He is truly a vampire. He has a small coven. They follow him, but he's lost interest in them. He—I don't want to repeat his name too much, because it empowers him, summons him. We have a history, you see."

"A history?" Aggie asked as she leaned forward.

"Yes, a painful history. You can probably imagine the worst and be close to the truth, but I survived with my life, which is why I know Patrice can too. But we need to move fast. I'll put in a call to Nathan. He might be able to help us with stopping him."

"If he was already on your radar, you must have had a plan already. Right?" Phoenix asked, his deep voice cracking slightly.

"My job was only to observe. I had no idea he would be trying to make a new convert. He often travels through the area, only to give speeches. He gets a kick out of preaching to mortals about the paranormal. It's a way to get into their community without being detected. I'm so sorry, Aggie. Now that we know he has Patrice in his sights, I fear the worst. The absolute worst."

Silent tears slid down Aggie's cheeks. She dug her phone out of her purse and tried to call her sister several times. Each time, it went to voicemail.

"I can't just sit by and let this happen. You must help us. Right, Phoenix? He has to help us find a way to save Patrice!"

"Let's meet up at the shop tonight after it closes. We need to set up some equipment and gather some more information. I'll do my best, Aggie. I swear to you I will."

Chapter Twelve—Aggie

The voice mailbox of the cell phone subscriber you are trying to reach is full. Please try again later. Goodbye.

I hung up for the umpteenth time and dropped the phone on the table in front of me. "Still no answer. It just keeps going straight to voicemail."

"She's got to come home at some point," Phoenix reassured me. "Maybe we should wait for her up there."

"I wouldn't be so sure she's coming home," I huffed. "She's been coming to the shop and the apartment less and less. I'm sure she knows that we are on to her by now. She *does* have her own abilities."

Mark paused. "Patrice also has abilities? What kind? Tell me about your sister."

"Empath, psychic. She's always had a sixth sense about things. I'm surprised she didn't pick up on Philip's past. She's usually very perceptive. You know, good at reading people. Growing up, she was perfect. She was always the perfect one. I used to get so ticked off with her. I am the oddball, and she's the good girl. Or so I thought."

"Maybe it's because she is such a good person, although perhaps inexperienced. Maybe that was why she was attracted to him. I get the feeling Philip prefers to dominate inexperienced women."

"Was? Could we please not speak about Patrice in the past tense?" That seemed rather rude.

"No one is giving up on her, Aggie. I promise." Phoenix offered some reassurance.

I took a deep breath and kept the conversation moving. "Patrice is like the rest of us, pretty new to these abilities. She sought guidance and found Philip. I'm not sure why. Maybe she has some weird connection to him or Esmine?"

Mark nodded in agreement. "All I know is that we've got to sever that connection and cut him out of her life. He's like a cancer that really needs to be removed."

My phone rang and startled me. It was Henri. "Hey, Henri."

"Aggie, Detra Ann and I wanted to check on you and Patrice. Everything okay?"

I tried to sound confident. "Yes, so far so good. I haven't seen Patrice yet. Phoenix has someone here that's a little more of an expert on what we are dealing with. His name is Mark. He works with a group called the Brotherhood."

Henri paused as if he wanted to say something. After a breath or two, he said, "Keep us posted on Patrice. She's like a daughter to us, as are you. We just want to make sure she's safe."

"Thanks so much. I'll be in touch as soon as I know something."

"Aggie, Detra Ann wants to stay out of this one, but if you need anything, anything at all, let me know. I will find a way to help you. Even if it's just to call in a friend. Maybe Carrie Jo or Ashland."

"Okay, I will. Thank you."

Phoenix touched my shoulder when I got off the phone. "Mark has everything set up."

"Do you think this is going to work?" I asked.

"Why wouldn't it? We've always come through before," he said with a wink. "Besides, it's got to."

I smiled. "You're right. I know I shouldn't worry, but I..."

"Can't help it," Phoenix interrupted. "I know."

His smile made my shoulders release. "Thanks."

"If you two are finished," Mark said as he walked in, "I've got all the equipment set up, and I called for backup. You never know what type of creature you're dealing with until they present themselves."

A familiar sound came from the back of the shop. It was the apartment door shutting.

Every muscle in my body tensed. "It's got to be Patrice."

"You know what to do," Phoenix whispered. "Let's go. We'll be right behind you."

The stairs creaked a little as we made our way up. I prayed that it wasn't enough to alert her to our presence.

I pushed the door open. "Patrice?"

No answer.

The doorknob clicked as I turned it and shut the door behind me. "Patrice?" I called out again, with no reply. Sweat gathered around my hairline and dripped down my temple. What if it *wasn't* her?

I looked down the dark hallway and held my breath with every step that drew me closer to her room.

Running my hand across the wall, I found the light switch. It clicked on and revealed an empty hallway. The door to

Patrice's room was slightly ajar. I pushed it open and braced myself.

Sitting on the bed with her back to me was the only person in the world who knew me completely. "Patrice?"

As she slowly turned toward me, she revealed my worst fear. Gaunt and drained of energy, she whispered, "Aggie."

"Yes, I'm here. Where have you been?"

"I... I..."

"Where's Philip?" I demanded. I can't say why, but my breathing was shallow. She kind of smiled, as if she knew I was having difficulty breathing. My hand went to my chest. Phoenix touched my shoulder.

"You okay?"

I ignored his question. "Philip, Patrice...where is he?" Her jaw snapped shut at the mention of Philip. I approached her cautiously and put my hand on her shoulder. "You've got to tell me. He's not who you think he is."

"You're wrong," Patrice whimpered. "You don't know anything about him, Aggie. Stay out of this. Why are you two here? Why are you ganging up on me? Who is that man behind you?"

"He's a friend. He's trying to help you see reason. This is Mark. I've had a vision. I used the ring you left behind, and I have proof that Philip Arnaud is a monster. He thinks you're his dead wife, Patrice! He thinks you are Esmine, and he wants to use you to bring her back. You have to know it's true!"

"I don't know that at all. He's here to protect me. He loves me, Aggie!" Patrice mustered enough strength to deny the truth. "You don't understand!"

I stepped closer to her. "He doesn't want to protect you. You know the truth. Deep down, you know." I couldn't help but sob. "Why else would you leave the ring here in your room? You knew I would find it and that I would see for myself. You want my help. Please, Patrice. Think about it." I spotted the antique mirror in her bag, grabbed it and shouted, "Look at what he's done to you, Patrice. He's already changing you to fit his needs. He is killing you!"

Patrice winced at the sight of her reflection. "That's not me. That's Esmine. My hair! My hair isn't right. This is some kind of trick, Aggie. What are you doing?"

"You know about Esmine?" I gasped. "What did he tell you? She killed herself, Patrice. She did it because she did not want to become like Philip. Look, we have to go! We have to go to a hospital, somewhere! Anywhere but here!"

Mark said, "The Brotherhood is waiting! They can help her. Come with us, Patrice. Please. It is a matter of life and death! Your life and death!"

My sister put up her hands and shook her head vigorously, as if she wanted to erase the truth. By doing so, it would make the truth go away. She did not look like herself at all. I tried not to cry, to bawl my eyes out. Her skin was so pale, I could see the green veins beneath them. Her eyes were sunken, despite the heavy makeup around them. She couldn't hide that. And her hair, it had become darker, much darker. Everything about her was changing. Almost before our very eyes.

"Philip told me how Esmine cursed him. This is her fault! She trapped his soul in the mirror, and he needs me to save him. I must break the spell. We must summon her, call her forth and call her out. I have to go to her."

I moved closer to my frantic sister. "No, Patrice. That's not it at all. Don't you know what he is doing? Do you know what the man is?"

Her eyes widened. "Of course I do. He's my soulmate. The only one who truly understands me. No one ever sees me. Not the real me! He is my lover, okay? He is my everything!"

"No!" I shook my head, my cheeks wet. "How can you believe that I am against you? I want you to be happy, but he is a monster! Literally, a monster. He's tricked you, Patrice. He is good at that. He has had centuries to learn how to do it. Philip is really a monster. A vampire! You've got to believe me. We've got to get you out of here before it is too late."

Mark intervened. "She is right, Patrice. Time is limited. We have to get you a transfusion, medications. I can help you with that. Please come with us."

Patrice didn't appear to be certain, although I could see she was torn. My sister loved me, but the monster's influence had taken hold. I reached my hand out to her, hoping and praying she would take it. To my relief, I saw that Patrice's face was beginning to soften. Her dark, sad eyes were watering with bloody tears.

Mark touched my shoulder. "I'll bring the car around and make that phone call. Let them know we're coming."

He and Phoenix disappeared from the room, I guess to leave us alone. To let us have a sisterly moment. I was happy about that.

Patrice licked her lips furiously. "I am so thirsty, Aggie."

"Would you like some water? A Coke, maybe?"

She turned her head away from me, her shoulders sagging strangely.

Oh, no! She's further gone than I first believed. Please, God! Don't let it be too late!

"Patrice!" I shouted. "You've got to come with me."

"No, I can't leave Philip. You don't understand. He needs me."

I took a step back. "I'm not leaving without you. You must trust me on this one, Patrice. There is still time. Please."

She closed her eyes. "Aggie, I do trust you. This is who I'm supposed to be. Phil—"

"Philip Arnaud is a monster. Don't you understand who he is? He's the undead. A bloodsucking creature. He only wants you because he thinks you are his dead wife! Wake up, Patrice! He doesn't want you—he wants Esmine! But I'll never give up on you. We will go, I promise. Together. We will go. I love you, sister."

Patrice screamed and said, "You are jealous! That's all. Philip told me you would say those things, and he was right. He does love me, Aggie."

A strange gust of wind blasted through the room. What was happening? No windows were open, and the air conditioning unit barely put out any cool air. This was not normal. Not at all.

"Monster?" Philip's laughter pierced through the dark corners of the room. "Tsk, tsk, Mary Agnes. You of all people should know that the paranormal world isn't always what it seems. Some may call me a monster; others see me as a savior."

I gagged at the momentary stench that followed the wind. An evil wind that brought the monster here. "Maybe I do not understand what you are exactly, but I know you are no savior. Far from it."

"Bravo!" He clapped his hands as the wind died down, taking the horrible smell with it. "It is so lovely to meet you. And to think, your sister wanted to keep you all to herself, didn't you, dear?"

Her shoulders slumped forward. The once-athletic body was now limp from exhaustion. Her hair hung in her face, and she wouldn't look at me anymore. I noticed her hands were clenched, clenched so tight that they had no color to them. None whatsoever.

"What have you done to Patrice? You can't have her! She is my sister. She's not Esmine, your dead wife, but you know that, don't you? You and I both know what lengths Esmine was willing to go to just to escape you. You are evil, Philip Arnaud. If that's even your real name."

Philip glared at me. "I have given Patrice life, purpose. She is mine now, little girl. Step away from her."

I grabbed Patrice by the arm and tugged her forward. "We've got to get you out of here, Patrice."

She stubbornly pulled away, her head still hanging down. I could feel her tensing, trembling. She was not going to listen to me.

"As you can see, she does not want to leave me. We are in love, and she has given her body and soul over to me, to fulfill her destiny. Why don't you come with us, Mary Agnes? We will be together, the three of us."

"Not a chance," I resisted. "Phoenix! Where are you?" I yelled at the top of my lungs.

"Pity. We could have made a wonderful trio." Philip's lips turned into a slit of a smile. His face reminded me of a snake, cool and controlled. His green eyes narrowed. They were piercing and anything but attractive.

Where are you, Phoenix?

Philip looked past me. "Are you looking for someone to save you? So much like your sister, Agnes. So much like many young women."

"I don't need anyone to save me. I'm perfectly capable of saving myself. You're not the first creep show that I've come across," I lied, trying to sound brave, but inside I was a bag of jelly. Was this guy reading my mind? Was that possible? "Shut up, creep!"

"That's not a very nice thing to say about your sister's soulmate. I may be a lot of things, but a creep isn't one of them. I don't stalk the helpless. I really do love Patrice, Agnes. Have you never been loved before? I think of her, dream about her, long for her. Has no one longed for you, dear Aggie?"

His words were smooth and sincere. This being actually believed that nothing was wrong with him. That he "loved" my sister, as he had "loved" Esmine, I supposed.

"I know who you are, and you won't get away with this. Patrice isn't going anywhere with you, not anymore. Whatever sick game you are playing, you've messed with the wrong person. I'm not going to let some bloodsucker ruin my family. Patrice, get behind me!" I shoved my sister behind me and reached for the only thing I could find, Patrice's blow dryer. Great, I was going to take on a powerful vampire with a blow dryer.

Philip moved closer and slapped it out of my hand with a frown. "Dear Aggie, you underestimate the paranormal again and again. Patrice is under my spell already. Just like Esmine.

There is nothing you can say or do to break that spell. Her love for me is deep."

I squeezed Patrice's hand and tried to get her to move. "You're not as powerful as you think you are." My voice was low, steady and determined. "You couldn't even hold on to Esmine, could you? She would rather burn than be yours. Have you told Patrice about your child? That Esmine gave birth to a monster. Is that what you want to do to Patrice? Have her bear your monsters?"

My words hit a nerve. The snarky grin disappeared from the devil of a creature. He raised his arms, showing the claws at the end of his long, pale fingers. The green in his eyes all but vanished into two dark discs surrounded by transparent flesh that exposed the absence of life. He growled deeply, like a wild animal.

Oh, crap! What have I done? Patrice whimpered behind me.

Philip cast a long shadow, and it appeared to grow and expand before my eyes. It hovered over my now-frozen body. I had to move and get us out of here. Now! Philip seemed to take up the whole space, blocking our every move. He lunged toward us. His claws extended, his long white teeth exposed.

"We've got to get out of here," I screamed at my sister. "Move, Patrice! We can't stay here. There's help in the shop, but we have to get down there together. I can't do this alone. I need you."

Patrice stared into my eyes. She had a look—a look of despair and sorrow. "I can't move, Aggie. His hands are on me. I can't get away. Run, Aggie. Run, while you can!"

I looked behind me but didn't see Philip, just the shadow that seemed to cover almost the entire room. Where was he? What was he doing?

"Yes, you can!" I shook her. "You are so strong, Patrice. You have always been strong. You can fight him. Fight, Patrice!" I was screaming at her now and trying to drag her out of the room. It was no use.

Patrice fell back onto the bed. "Just leave me," she sobbed. "He has me, Aggie. He has me forever."

"No," I refused. "That's not an option. I am not leaving you."

"It's too late for me. His voice..." Patrice grabbed her head between her hands. "I can't get his voice out of my head. He won't leave me alone."

"Don't let him win! Stay with me! You've got to stay with me."

Where were Mark and Phoenix?

Chapter Thirteen—Patrice

Philip stood behind Aggie now. Didn't she feel him? Didn't he make her body tingle? My body was tingling all over, and I was so thirsty. I needed a drink.

Soon, my love. Soon.

Philip emerged from the shadow completely. I could see Aggie's face, her eyes wide, her lips not moving. I rose from the bed, unsure what to do.

"We all know what an inadequate, ugly duckling you are, Aggie. You have been so jealous of your sister for such a long time. We have talked about it often, haven't we, Patrice? You know, Aggie, it's a shame that you couldn't hide your contempt for your sister just this once to let her have this moment of happiness."

I couldn't speak. I wouldn't speak. No, I never said that. I never believed that. What was Philip doing? Why would he be so cruel to Aggie?

"Patrice?" Aggie's eyes filled with tears.

"Sister," I whispered silently.

"I always wanted you to be happy. I love you. I am sorry, Patrice."

For a moment, I remembered the little girl who followed me around, my shadow, who always wanted to be like me. I did not hate her for any of that. Philip was wrong. He was so very wrong.

I walked past them both, glancing at the mirror that hung on the wall. The reflection staring back at me looked different. Yes, I had changed. My eyes followed the outline of the reflection in the mirror.

This wasn't me at all. Who am I?

The clothes and hairstyle were different. Esmine stared back at me. Her black dress and veil highlighted her pale skin and glowing eyes. How was this possible? This wasn't the hand mirror...this was my mirror. I moved my hand in front of it, swaying it from left to right. Esmine did the opposite. Her eyes were pleading with mine. I gasped.

Aggie was sobbing, but I could not comfort her. I had to distract Philip. I had to do it now. If I set him free, he would go. He would leave us alone. I loved him, but I loved my sister more. I loved my life. I didn't want this. I did not want to become someone else.

Philip came to me, his whispers echoing in my ears. "Can you see her? Isn't she lovely? Just like you. So much like you, Patrice."

Unable to speak, I stretched out my hand to the ghostly reflection. Philip's gaze turned toward the mirror.

His green eyes widened. "Esmine!" he said with as much longing as I've ever heard. Esmine's face changed. It became an image of hatred. Oh yes, she hated him. Hated him completely. Her image slowly faded, and she moved across the mirror and disappeared from our view.

"Where did she go?" he shouted, investigating the surroundings. His hands motioned toward the mirror, which now had no reflection. "She was just here, within my grasp." Philip stared at the empty space. "Bring her back! Summon her back, Patrice!"

"I..I... don't know how," I confessed desperately.

"You bring her back." He grabbed my shoulders, enraged. "You bring her back now!"

I cried, "Philip, I don't know how. I thought it was my reflection at first. We...look so much alike. What have you done to me?" What little strength I had left began to fade. Reality struck me. His love for Esmine had never died. Maybe Aggie had been right?

My heart burst into a million pieces, and a cold darkness came over me.

No, he never loved me. It was always her. Always Esmine. Visions of them together flooded my mind. Living as man and wife and loving one another. Until she knew the truth. I couldn't look in his eyes. I knew the truth. Really, I did.

"You don't love me, do you?"

Philip grasped my chin, squeezing my mouth closed, his lips curled in a snarl and his eyes narrowed. "My dear, you were just the means to an end. I need you to bridge the gap. To bring my Esmine back to me. No one could ever replace her. I love her. When I said forever, I meant it."

"Let her go," Aggie said as she collected herself. She reached for something; I couldn't see what it was this time. Philip's hands were firmly around my throat, but this strange thirst took control of me. I pulled at his hands, snapped at them with my teeth.

"I wouldn't do that if I were you." Philip snapped his head toward her. "And if your sister comes any closer, I'll break her neck."

"Aggie, do what he says," I growled angrily. Yes, I was angry. Angry at myself for allowing this thing to control me. To put me and my sister in danger. How could I have been so blind? I needed to distract him. Buy us some time. Surely Mark and Phoenix would return, wouldn't they? "Why did you need *me*? Why me, Philip?"

Philip gurgled an evil laugh. "You and Esmine are kindred spirits. Your soul called out to mine. I knew that you were her twin soul as soon as I saw you in the crowd that day. It's more than a resemblance, more than appearance. She is truly your sister—you are a part of her. I've searched for you for years."

"Searched for years? How did you find me?" I questioned him, looking for a way to distract him. "Maybe you were meant to be with me and not Esmine."

"Not Esmine? Patrice, wake up," Aggie huffed. "I can't believe you're still thinking this guy is in love with you."

She had no idea what I was doing, and I couldn't take time to explain it.

Philip released his hold of me. "What we have has nothing to do with love, my dear. Desire, yes. Love, no. Do you think that Esmine's belongings just happened to show up in your antiques store for no reason? I knew they would find you."

This was all so insane. "How would those objects find me? Are they haunted? Are they attached to me? What did you do to me?"

His answer was a smile, an evil smile. The air practically crackled with electricity. I could smell blood, blood everywhere. My mouth was so dry. I needed a drink. A deep drink.

Yes, I know you feel the hunger. You could take her. You could drink her dry.

"Stop it, Philip! I'll never do that!"

"What's he talking about? What's going on? Patrice, come with me now!"

I saw Aggie easing toward the door, but she clearly wasn't willing to leave me behind. I was terrified for her, but also for me. What was I capable of? Rage welled up within me. I wanted to kill him—kill someone.

"I'm sure Aggie understands what I mean. Don't you, Agnes?"

My sister sobbed but didn't back down. Finally, she confessed, "I had a vision, Patrice. Esmine killed herself when Philip turned her into one of his kind. He must have put some sort of curse on her and her belongings. To help him find her in the afterlife. But we can't be sure. He's a liar, Patrice."

"Smart girl," Philip said with a sneer. "You've been studying, haven't you? Now let's see how smart you are, Aggie." He grabbed me again, and my flesh burned with desire for him still, but the thirst was growing. "Bring her back to me, Patrice. Only you can do it. You're not strong enough now, but soon you will be. You should drink her blood. Drink and be strong!"

Aggie screamed at me, "No, Patrice! Don't listen to him! You have to fight! Phoenix!"

My body trembled from the coldness that began to radiate from my stomach. Hands shaking and feet numb from the ungodly temperature, I tried to reach out for Philip. "What's happening to me?"

A guttural laugh escaped him as he replied, "You are beginning your new life. One that we will share with Esmine. When your soul turns, the connection will be strong enough to bring her spirit back into your body. We will live together forever."

"You mean to kill me. You want to give my body to Esmine."

Aggie cried at hearing that. I couldn't make a sound.

"You will be among the damned. Always watching but never dying. You will only be able to watch Esmine and me surrender to our love. But you will never sleep again." The coldness enveloped me, and the world turned to darkness with Aggie's screams in my ears. "It will be worth it, sweet Patrice. Let me show you what we once shared. Let me show you why I need you."

I felt myself swirling up, up and up.

Chapter Fourteen—Esmine

The noise of Paris had been drowned out by the clanking of the carriage wheels and horses' hooves that carried us deep into the countryside. Away from the chaos that had stabbed at the heart of our way of life. Whispers of another revolt had put us all into an anxious, wary state.

"Fresh air will do us all good," Papa said. "My cousin Pierre has a place for us. No fear, ladies. All will be well."

After our hurried escape, the days did move more slowly. Life in the country was safer, quieter, but I so enjoyed the company of the city. No souls to speak of were out here in the fields of lavender. Eventually, the rows of dark purple did nothing to lift my spirits. No, only lively music and dances would do to soothe my young soul. My youth was coming to an end within this cruel, dark world. Or so I believed.

"Esmine," Mama interrupted my daydream, "come back to us, dear child." She laughed playfully.

"My apologies, Mama. I suppose I was daydreaming. I do miss the city. When will we return to Paris?"

Mama and Papa exchanged a knowing look. They could speak without saying a word. I wanted a love like that, someone who I could spend my life with maybe never saying a word. Just knowing. There would be no such person out here in the countryside. Who would I find amongst the trees and bales of hay?

"We just arrived, mon petite. Now is not the time for this," Papa replied sternly. "You are getting old enough to think of others, not just yourself. Our family needs to be away from the dreadful city. Can't you see what is happening?"

Mama shared a sour expression with him and took the conversation in a different direction. "There's too much going on there. Too much. We will go home one day. Have patience, Esmine."

They were right, of course. I was thinking only of myself. I knew Papa worried about our family and what would become of us. The aristocracy was seen as the enemy, and our way of life had been challenged by the continual uprisings. Would France ever be at peace again?

Our extended family had been scattered across Europe to escape the atrocities. I felt pity for the bourgeoisie. They were merely trying to better themselves, but at what cost? Would they rather everyone fall to their knees? There would always be a hierarchy in civilizations. We were all handed our destiny at birth, each with its own difficulties. I knew this; I learned quite well from my old tutor.

"I do apologize, Papa," I answered meekly. "I do think of the family. I know we are safer away from Paris."

Mama smiled suspiciously. "Besides, there is something wonderful to think about, Esmine. The Marquis de Cheverny is hosting an extravagant soiree for you. You are hailed as quite the beauty, even here in the countryside. For now, you will have to satisfy yourself with dancing with the Marquis and his sons." A sly grin spread across her face. "There will be guests there from all around Europe. You will not be too far from your beloved dancing and music. See? Your wish has come true."

I hugged Mama before stealing an apple from the bowl between us. I rose to my feet and swung my skirts around in a faux dance. Suddenly, the day seemed brighter, more vivid. The air felt crisper. Then I pelted Mama with questions. "Who will be there? What should I wear?"

A few days later, we were winging our way to the elegant chateau. The road to the chateau wound through trees so tall that they blocked out the sun. It was an ancient forest, dark and mysterious. I dare say you could not see farther than a few feet through it. A familiar scent tickled my nose, one that reminded me of my hope chest that had traveled along with us.

Sweet and warm.

We passed through the long line of cedar trees before entering the opening, exposing the stone home set beyond the forest. It was a lovely, grand home. Imposing and intricate carvings were above each window and door; the carvings stood out against the pale stone facade.

An elderly gentleman met us outside along the path that ran in front of the lovely home. "Bienvenue," he said with a snap of his head. "The Marquis de Cheverny has been expecting you. We have prepared your rooms. The soiree will begin within the hour. You have plenty of time to freshen up."

Taking in the spectacle of it all, I couldn't help but think, what a lovely prison to be captured in. It was a gilded cage. Something I had become quite used to. The interior was no different. An enormous parlor greeted us. It was filled with paintings of the many aristocrats who had spent their lives here.

Melodic notes floated through the air, echoing through the hallways, bouncing off the many artifacts that clung to the stone walls. I broke away from our entourage, determined to find this treasure. I loved music. I ignored Mama, who insisted on calling me to her side, as if I were her pet poodle.

As the music got louder, my heart began to reach up into my throat. The piano gently summoned me to come closer. The music tinkled and then took on an intensity that strummed at my very soul.

I pushed open the ivory-colored door trimmed in gold. Large oil paintings hung on all the muted yellow walls. Louis XVI furniture was scattered around the room facing the corner. And perched in that corner behind the grand piano was the most handsome creature I had ever laid eyes on. His head moved to the music in a trancelike state, flowing along with the melody.

As I moved closer to him, I could see his hands moving along the ivory, caressing each note with great fervor. I was enraptured. His solitary performance captured me. I began to feel like an intruder who had stepped within the boundaries of a magical, hidden world. My feet would not move away from this magnificence.

Enthralled, I stood mesmerized by the scene.

The music stopped, and my heart froze as his piercing green eyes found mine. I couldn't look away or run. Nor did I want to. I felt seen for the first time. The very first time. He looked deep into my soul, beyond this earthly flesh. Into my very heart.

Catching my breath to break the silence, I said, "My apologies, monsieur. I just heard the music, and I had come to see."

He lifted his hand. "No need to apologize to me. It is I who should apologize. I get lost sometimes within my own thoughts once the music starts to flow from me."

"Your playing is beautiful, sir. I have never heard such an enchanting song. Who is the composer?"

"I've had years of practice. The song is my own," he said with a laugh. "I'm Philip Arnaud." He pushed away from the piano bench, stood, and held out his hand.

I held my hand out for him. "I'm Esmine de la Fontaine."

His lips gently kissed my hand. "It is a pleasure to meet you."

"How do you know the Marquis?" I asked as I pretended my hand didn't burn with his touch, despite the coolness of his lips.

Philip's smile widened. "We are old friends. I'm here for the soiree. I do love a good party. I hope you will be staying as well. But then again, it is all for you, isn't it?"

"Yes, I hear that it is. Will you be staying at the chateau for long?"

His smile dissipated. "Troubles in Paris. I think everyone with good taste will be here."

"Yes, unfortunately. My hope is that something good will happen soon."

"What good would that be?" he asked as his eyes studied me.

I wanted to leap into his arms and never leave. I really didn't know. His smile and eyes, I had never seen such. Every inch of him called out to me. Nothing mattered anymore besides this complete stranger. He consumed me. I wanted to know this Philip Arnaud.

He smoothed back one strand of hair. "There are some who think that there is balance in life. Bad comes with good and vice versa. It seems to all work together within this world of ours. Without the bad, there would be no way of knowing what is good. Correct?"

"Wise words for such a young man who has only just begun living." I smiled bravely, hoping my guess was correct. He could be no older than twenty-five, surely.

Philip's eyes softened. "What if I told you that I have lived a dozen lifetimes in this young, vigorous body? There is not much that I've not seen or gone through. Each time, a new lesson has been learned and implemented."

"You speak as if you've really lived more than one life," I scoffed. "I think you are toying with me, sir. We only have this one life to live."

He moved closer to me. "There are some who close their eyes to what is possible and see only what they want to see regarding this life. We all have a destiny to fulfill, that is true." He took his hand in mine, and his lips gently pressed against it once more in a slow kiss. "But there are many paths to follow to get to our ultimate destination."

Philip released my hand. I watched in silence as he left the room and disappeared into the great hall.

I wanted to run after him.

Embrace him and never let go.

In my soul, I knew that he *was* my destiny.

Fight him. Resist him. He is an evil man.

Esmine? Is that you? What must I do?

Lead him to me, Patrice. Lead him to me. I will help you. Trust me...

I want to, but I don't want to die. Am I going to die?

The woman who looked like me began to weep. Her face was in her hands. I understood the answer to my question. We were trapped, Esmine and I. Trapped along with Philip. The three of us. Forever tied together. I could not let this happen to Aggie. I had to save her—save them all.

Save us.

I will do it, Esmine. I will do it...

Chapter Fifteen—Phoenix

The invisible force that blocked our reentry into the apartment lifted, and Mark and I tumbled in. Things were a blur. Activity bustled around us, although there was nothing to see. Still, I couldn't pretend I didn't feel many hands on me, many eyes watching me.

As if he read my mind, Mark shouted at me, "Ignore them! They can't touch you!" Mark tugged at his necklace to reveal a large cross pendant. I suddenly wished I had one of those. I allowed him to take the lead, and we raced toward Patrice's room.

I will never in my life forget the sight that met me. Aggie was on the floor, bleeding from her mouth, and her eye appeared bruised. Obviously, she'd been flung out of the way of the creature. Yes, Philip Arnaud had transformed into a creature! His thick, dark hair revealed pointed ears and a strangely twisted face with yellow teeth. There was nothing handsome about him, nothing attractive at all. Worse than anything was the sight of Patrice's limp body in his oddly long arms. I couldn't say for sure, but she appeared to be dead.

"Patrice!" I screamed without thinking.

Aggie moaned in response. "Phoenix, help her!" she implored me as she wiped the blood from her mouth with the back of her hand.

I wanted to, but how? Patrice's eyes were closed, but I thought perhaps I saw them flutter. Was she alive? Was she playing dead?

"Put her down!" Mark yelled at the Philip-monster. "Now! You cannot have her, Arnaud! We know what you're trying to do. Esmine is beyond your grasp. Gone forever. Let Patrice go!"

"As you wish," he replied as he dumped her on the floor. Patrice rolled as she fell and landed on her face. Aggie tried to crawl to her, but I pulled her back. My skin crawled, and I felt sick to my stomach. Something was wrong with Patrice. She moved awkwardly, thrashed about as if she were having a seizure. Aggie struggled against me, but I prevailed. At least for the moment. She sobbed against my shoulder. I couldn't stop staring at Philip Arnaud.

This whole situation was going south quick. The room wasn't big enough for four people and a vampire. Or whatever the hell this man had become. Was he a vampire or something else? Mark held up his cross and babbled something. A blessing? A spell? Again, how could I know?

Patrice flipped over awkwardly. It was a weird movement, like an invisible pair of hands tossed her around. Her eyes opened, and she sat up as stiff as a board. Oh, God! Patrice was beginning to change, to turn. Would she become a creature like Philip Arnaud? How was this possible? I felt like I was in the middle of a horror movie.

Aggie struggled against me. She wanted to go to Patrice, to rescue her, but I was pretty sure she was beyond our help.

Mark yelled at us, "Leave her be! She's becoming one of them."

Patrice turned her head stiffly. Her eyes were not as they had been, not expressive and sweet. They were yellow and narrow, just like Philip Arnaud's.

Patrice screamed as Philip laughed. She was breathing as he was, quickly, like a panting dog.

"No, Patrice! Come with me! It's Aggie! I'm your sister!"

Patrice began to crawl toward us with a monstrous grin slapped across her face. It was a terrible thing to see—this once-beautiful woman shifting into a monster straight from hell. Without hesitation, Patrice swung her arm and lunged at Aggie. My girlfriend screamed in terror as she practically climbed on top of me.

Mark slid between us, shoving his cross in her direction. He wasn't mumbling anymore but yelling in Latin. At least, I assumed it was Latin. Philip roared in anger as Patrice swung back and away from us. She sobbed, like a human. Like herself.

Aggie whispered to her, "Fight, Patrice! Fight him! Please!" Although I wanted to believe that Patrice had a chance to remain human, I couldn't be sure, and I refused to let Aggie move closer.

Patrice whimpered; a bloody tear trickled down her cheek. "I-can't-Aggie...I-can't! I love y—." And then she began to growl again. She growled like a rabid dog. Suddenly, my eyes were drawn to the oversized mirror that hung over Patrice's fireplace. It was a beautiful faux vintage mirror with an elegant frame.

I whispered to Aggie, "Look at the mirror. Look, Aggie."

Mark began to chant even louder, pushing Philip back. To my surprise, the powerful creature responded to Mark's prayers.

It didn't like what he was doing, not at all. Patrice continued to flail like a fish out of water.

"Patrice, come to me! Come now!" Philip commanded her as she rose to her feet. Patrice wobbled back and forth, as if at any moment she would fall over. He didn't see the ghost of Esmine, but judging from Mark's determined expression, I believed Mark saw her.

"No! Hold her, Phoenix! Hold Patrice or we will lose her!"

"What?" I couldn't believe what he was asking me to do. How was I going to restrain this snarling half-creature?

"Help me, Phoenix!" Aggie grabbed her sister from behind. She slid her arms under Patrice's and immediately fell backward. The sisters hit the floor with a loud thud. Aggie yelped in pain, but she refused to let Patrice go. I couldn't hesitate. If I did, I could lose Aggie. It was then that I realized how much I loved her. I did love Aggie. I'd loved her from the first moment I met her at Devecheaux Antiques. In school, our paths didn't cross much. How could I have missed her?

I kept my eye on the mirror as I came to Aggie's aid. She was holding Patrice, who was kicking at me, struggling and babbling in a weird language. Mark waved his cross at her as Philip stepped back, closer to the mirror and away from the power that my friend wielded. I wasn't a religious person, but I had to admit that there was clearly strength and authority in Mark's faith.

Patrice settled down, and I slid Aggie out of the way and took her place. We continued to keep Patrice's arms pinned behind her to keep her from scratching at Aggie. Oddly, Patrice began to weaken. I could feel her strength fading. Her body relaxed, but it could be a trick. Maybe she wanted me to believe that so I'd let her go. No, that wasn't going to happen.

Philip stormed toward Mark and struck the smaller man with the back of his oversized hand. "Give me Patrice! Give her to me! She is mine! Forever! I will kill you! I will eat you—devour you! Piece by piece!"

"No!" Mark roared back. "She is not yours!" But Mark had the wind knocked out of him.

Philip wavered momentarily, but he wasn't going to stay that way forever. He put his hand around Mark's throat and slowly lifted him from the floor.

"I will kill you slowly; you and all the Brotherhood! What fools you are to believe you can stop me. I am older than your country. Older than you can imagine. Today, you die!" He opened his mouth and showed his yellowed teeth.

Mark gurgled my name. "Phoenix, take it. The cross..." The last word ended with a terrible hiss.

I knew what he wanted. He wanted me to grab the cross and push Philip toward the mirror. The vampire hadn't noticed the ghost yet, but she was becoming clearer by the minute. Her dark hair and pale skin were fleshed out. Her dark eyes watched as Philip put his mouth to Mark's throat. I had no confidence in my ability to use the religious artifact correctly, but what choice did I have?

"Aggie! Take her!" I ordered as I let go of Patrice, but the woman didn't react. Her eyes were closed, her body still. It was as if she were truly dying this time. I snatched up the cross and jumped to my feet. Without thinking, I raised it as I'd seen Mark do. "Back, Philip! Let him go and get back!"

Philip paused his assault; he'd only broken the skin. It wasn't bleeding much. I wanted to run away and wet myself at the same time, but I wasn't able to do either. Philip didn't release Mark. The man continued to gasp for air, his color changing to a light pale, almost blue. That wasn't good. Not good at all.

Philip's yellow eyes shifted to mine. He hated me. I could see his hate, feel his hate. He hated me, but he also wasn't sure about me. Wasn't sure I had the authority I needed to hold the cross. What if he challenged me? Would God back me up?

"Move back! Let him go!"

To my complete surprise, Philip Arnaud tossed Mark on the bed and faced me. He laughed at me; it was a terrible, animalistic sound. "I'll kill you first. My Patrice will enjoy tasting you—and then her sister!"

I sobbed at his threat but didn't lower the cross. I took another step toward him, and despite his horrible words, he fell back against the fireplace.

Esmine's arms reached through the mirror. Unlike the apparition in the mirror, the arms were skeletal. Skeletal and strong. Strong enough to catch Philip off guard.

"My baby! You made my baby a monster!" she hissed at him. "I shall end you, husband. I shall end you forever..." her scratchy voice threatened as she tugged at him. Esmine lifted him off his feet, and he screamed in surprise.

"Esmine! Don't do this. I will bring you back..."

And then in less than five seconds, Philip Arnaud was transforming, no more a monster. No more a handsome man. He was old and rotten. I could see him clearly in the mirror, see him as he truly was without his immortal curse.

Esmine towered over him as he fell to the ground, too ancient and weak to exert any strength over her. She wore a black dress with a high collar. Her long, dark hair hung around her, hiding her face. She did not weep for him. She did not speak to him except to say, "Now you die. Forever."

Philip continued to sag and then disintegrate. He became a rotten pile of bones and then powder. Esmine turned to face me. She saw me, and her dark eyes were so much like Patrice's that I couldn't stop staring. Esmine took a step closer to me. I was mesmerized by her, by what just happened.

Suddenly, something flew by me. A lamp? It struck the oversized mirror, which shattered into a hundred pieces. I covered my face and waited for the crashing to end. Mark pulled me by the back of my shirt, and together we fell on the bed. Mirror shards were everywhere, but Esmine was gone—and so was Philip Arnaud.

Aggie cried over her sister. Patrice would not wake up. Aggie tapped her face with her hand. "Patrice! Wake up! It's over—it's all over!"

And I knew it was true. It was all over for Patrice. Whatever hold Philip had on her, whatever magic he used, it had been enough to kill her. Patrice was dead. Truly dead.

Ignoring the broken mirror, I kneeled by Aggie's side as she continued to cry...

Chapter Sixteen—Aggie

Patrice's favorite dress lay across the bed. It was black with pink polka dots, a Peter Pan collar and a thin pink belt. This would be the last outfit I would ever help her choose. Our mother couldn't do it. She clung to her rosary, hoping for some miracle, and our father was devoid of any emotion but anger. Anger that was directed at me. I couldn't explain to them what happened. Not completely. Not honestly. The coroner concluded Patrice died of heart failure, but there was no explanation for the wounds on her neck. The strange condition of her skin. The sudden and unexpected white streak in her hair.

Of course, they questioned all of us, but our story was the same. An intruder must have broken in and scared Patrice to death. Whoever it was had escaped, and the guy was on the run. End of story. We covered our tracks as well as we could. Only time would tell if the police believed it.

I was numb.

There was a space in the pit of my stomach that just couldn't be filled. Patrice was gone, and there was nothing I could do about it. That last day together had been a sheer nightmare. Philip was gone, but he had taken Patrice with him. Somehow, it was true.

I picked up the dress and held it in my arms, inhaling her scent one last time. I knew the perfume she wore, but I would never use it. I'd boxed it up along with her other personal items. I wasn't going to keep them—I'd give them to Mom. I did keep a few things, things I knew she wanted me to have. Like her Mickey Mouse wallet and her silver charm bracelet. But it would be a long time before I held them or used them. I couldn't fight the guilt I felt. The absolute, undeniable guilt.

Driving over to the funeral home, I thought of all the events that had led up to this tragedy. I should have asked more questions. Confronted Patrice sooner. Demanded to meet the unholy Philip Arnaud. I should never have asked her to move in with me or work at the shop. It was too much. Too much for Patrice, too much for me. My parents were right—it *was* all my fault. I mean, they didn't say it to my face, but every sigh, every expression, every unsaid word was an accusation. I couldn't blame them.

Someone had to take the blame, and it had to be me.

The funeral home was cold and quiet, as they always were. I hated funerals. Low chatter filled the separate rooms as Patrice's friends gathered. People from high school and college. The popular kids. The smart ones. They wept and cried. How could this happen? How could Patrice, who was so smart and beautiful, die from a heart attack?

Their praise of Patrice, how she was kind-hearted and beautiful, it was true. All of it was true. She had been the epitome of the all-American girl, but more than that, she'd been my hero. I'd always wanted to be her. Always. I passed through the crowds of people. They were all solemn and sincere. Each stopped me and offered their condolences.

I politely thanked them, as anyone would. I held the scream that I desperately wanted to release deep within my chest. I wanted to hit someone. Punch them. I wished I could punch myself. My parents kept the casket closed, which was a welcomed and wise choice. I couldn't have stood to see Patrice like that. Dead and broken. Like a flimsy rag doll.

"Aggie." Phoenix tapped me on the shoulder. His impeccably fitted suit was a change from his typical jeans and t-shirt. It suited him well. I was so glad to see him.

"Phoenix," I said through trembling lips. I wrapped my arms around him and held on tight. He was all I had left. I melted into him. The warmth of his body felt like a comforting blanket.

He kissed me on the forehead. "How are you holding up, Aggie?"

I looked up. "I'm glad you're here."

He squeezed my hand protectively as he surveyed the crowd. "She knew a lot of people," he said, looking around the room. "I forgot how popular she'd been. I mean is. I mean..."

"It's okay, Phoenix. Yes, people loved Patrice. She lit up any room she was in. It's ironic that her life ended in such a dark space."

Phoenix loosened his hold on my hand. "Your parents seem to be doing okay. Are they talking to you yet?"

I glanced over at them sitting on the couch by the casket, surrounded by pink roses and daisy arrangements. "They are better today. It's been a difficult week. We don't really have much to say."

"Are they still asking questions?"

"Not so much anymore. We did have a detective stop by yesterday. Of course, there were no updates on the killer. But I don't think they will ever stop looking. They had questions about the mirror."

Phoenix brushed my hair out of my face. "Why? We know that they will never find him, but they don't know that. What's the harm in them looking?"

My stomach churned. "The harm would be in if they actually found out what happened. It would kill my parents because then they would really believe it's my fault."

"Sooner or later, you've got to tell them who you are. You know that, right?"

I pulled away from him. "I'll tell them when the time is right. It's not now, Phoenix."

"I know you will, and you're probably right."

The gray casket stood out amid the black-clothed attendees. Bagpipes played *Amazing Grace*, and for a moment, I was lost within the melody. Away from the reality of it all.

How could she have left us so soon? How could I have let her down so completely?

Lively music filled the air, intermingled with the smell of beer and pizza. Food was the last thing on my mind. It had been three weeks since Patrice's funeral, but it felt like a million years. When had I eaten last? Or showered? Or done anything productive? Why had I agreed to come here? Oh yeah, Phoenix.

It was a crowded Friday night, and this was the last place I wanted to be. But Phoenix had insisted, so here I was, out in the world that I had no desire to be a part of. At all.

"Hey, Aggie." Phoenix pulled out a chair. "I was beginning to think you weren't going to come."

I shrugged as I sat down and tried to get comfortable in the wooden chair. "You make it hard to say no."

He leaned in for a sweet kiss. "I'm glad you showed up. You need to get out of the house. It's been three weeks."

"It's hard to be here."

His hand touched mine. "I think I know what will get your mind off of things. You need to get back in the game, Ags. Mark and I have been working on our website. He should be here any minute to show you what we've come up with."

Getting back in the game had not been on my radar. Actually, that was the last thing I wanted to do. Whatever "getting back in the game" meant. I wanted no part of it.

"I'm not ready, Phoenix. It's too much, too soon."

Phoenix leaned back in his chair. "There's never a good time to do this, but I know you want to help people. Think about all the people out there that need our help. People like Patrice." *Why? Why did he have to mention her name?*

Phoenix shifted in his seat. "Mark and I want to start a project together. An ongoing project. The Society of the Supernatural. It's like an S.O.S. call. You know if you're in trouble, call us. Kind of thing."

"That's clever. You come up with that all on your own?" I almost smiled just because of the name. "I thought you were a creative songwriter."

"Ouch. That hurt," he said, grabbing his stomach as if I'd punched him in the gut. "You really know how to wound someone's ego."

"It's been a little while, but I still have it," I answered dryly.

"That's the Aggie I know and love. Welcome back."

"Thanks, but I'm not actually back yet."

Phoenix ordered us two beers, but I passed on the food. "Have you heard from Henri or Detra Ann?"

He tapped the table nervously. "Yes, they called me a few days ago to check on me. Detra Ann is being supportive. Totally understanding. She gave me paid time off, but to tell you the truth, I don't know what I want to do. Stay? Go? I'm not sure." My throat started to close, and I pressed my lips together.

I had stayed away from anything that might cause a paranormal event. The room at my parents' house had been a sanctuary for me, away from the world. Patrice's room had been locked up, and no one was allowed to step over the threshold. Her belongings had been put in there as a sort of shrine.

"I'm sorry, but I truly think that this will help you decide. At least hear me out." His voice was warm and comforting. I knew he meant well.

"I'll listen. I might even try, but if things start to go sideways again or if anyone is in danger, I'm out. I can't handle losing anyone else. Understood?"

"Understood."

"Well, looks like you two started the meeting without me," Mark said as he put his laptop on the table and plopped down beside me. He hugged me and asked how I was doing. I smiled but didn't have much to say. I'm sure he could guess. "Did Phoenix tell you the name of our little group?"

"He did," I replied, but I still didn't want to commit to anything.

"Society of the Supernatural. Sounds like some '90s bar band or something, right?" Mark chuckled. "But it's catchy."

"I like '90s bar bands," I scoffed. "Besides, I think the name has a ring to it. People will get the meaning behind it."

"I guess." Mark opened his laptop. "Here's what the website looks like so far. There's some info about us, what we do and how to get in contact with us."

"Looks good," Phoenix replied.

"When does it go live?" I asked.

"It will be ready to roll tonight," Mark answered with far too much excitement. Didn't he remember what we just went through?

"Sounds good," I lied. Really, I wasn't ready at all. But this was my calling, wasn't it? And as cliche as it may sound, I had to try again. Try to help others. My sister's death should mean something. I should do more than hide in my old bedroom. I knew I needed to get back to life.

I had an apartment to decide about. A job to decide about. The worst had happened—I lost my sister. But what about other sisters? Other men, women, boys and girls?

I excused myself and scurried off to the restroom. For the first time since the funeral, I cried my eyes out. I cried so hard a stranger put her arm around me and offered me a tissue. When I left the ladies' room, I was committed to keep going. To keep seeking. To keep working.

Walking to the table, I felt like a new person. A broken person but one with a renewed commitment.

I sat down at the table and tossed my purse beside me. "I'm all in, guys. I'm all in."

There would be no turning back.

Epilogue—Henri

A dark shadow had hovered over our antiques shop since Patrice's death. Aggie, Phoenix and Mark explained to me what happened, but I asked them to keep it to themselves. "Please don't tell my wife. She's not ready to hear this. I'll keep it to myself, but don't tell her."

"We will honor your wishes, Henri. I'll protect Detra Ann from this." Aggie hugged my neck, and I hugged her back.

She was truly like my own kid. Detra Ann loved her too. My wife was like that. She got attached to people quickly. Especially good people, like Aggie. Patrice had been good too, but in the end, she'd gotten mixed up with the wrong man. Not just a troubled man, an evil man. But a vampire? I would never have guessed.

I sighed as I unboxed the latest shipment of antiques. These were from another shop; Lamont Owens, a friend in New Orleans, often sold us his overstock. They weren't always the best pieces, but this box promised to be a good one. I lifted a lantern out of the packing peanuts. Unlike flame lanterns such as candle or oil lamps, gas lanterns relied on heated mantles that created light. The first commercial use of gas lighting was in 1792 by a man called William Murdoch. Lanterns and lamps were kind of my thing. I knew more than I should about them. I'd always found them fascinating. Gas lanterns were developed during the 19th century, and portable lanterns like this one used kerosene as a fuel. It had a control knob that adjusted the brightness and turned off the lantern. Eventually, gas lanterns were replaced by electric ones.

After a quick examination, I removed the rest of the items: a beautiful embroidered shawl embellished with gold thread, a useless set of ceramic roosters and an interesting silver condiment holder. Now, I liked that. It was certainly from the 18th century.

I took the empty box to the back door. We'd learned to keep quite a few of them on hand because our online sales were growing. Business had been slow today. Detra Ann and I worked constantly because of Patrice's passing and Aggie's need to take time off. I couldn't believe Patrice was gone. Such a bright light gone too soon. I hoped Aggie stayed with us, but I would completely understand if she didn't. It would be hard to live in that apartment, to work at Devecheaux Antiques. Yeah, I was ready to go home. It was only fifteen minutes early. My wife normally wouldn't approve, but I was pretty sure she would be happy to see me today.

I flicked off the light in the workroom, but something was wrong. The lamp was glowing! The kerosene lamp glowed a bright light. Then a dim light. It went bright and then dim three times. I flipped the switch back on and went back to my workbench. There was no way this lamp could glow. It had no kerosene. It didn't even have a wick in it!

I took the lamp apart, but everything I found confirmed my assumption. This wasn't right. This wasn't right at all.

Holy crap! Not again. We didn't need this to happen again. How was it that strange items kept making their way to us?

To Devecheaux Antiques? I sure as heck wasn't going to tell my wife about this today. Maybe I would tomorrow, or the day after that. But for sure not today.

I decided to move everything away from the lamp. I wasn't taking any chances. I didn't want the place to catch on fire because of a ghost lamp. *Great. Ghost lamp. I've named it.*

Well, this was one item I'd take care of myself. Or send back. I wasn't sure yet. Yeah, sending it back was probably the best idea. We'd been through enough. But even as I thought that, the reassembled light flickered again. Only momentarily this time.

"Who's here?" I asked in the empty store. I didn't hear a sound. Not a voice, not a peep. Nothing to make me think someone was pulling a prank on me. And who would do that? To my surprise, the phone rang. I swore softly under my breath as I went to the front of the store to answer it.

"Devecheaux Antiques, Henri speaking. How may I help you?"

"Hey, Henri. It's Lamont. Calling to make sure you received the items I sent you."

"Uh, yeah. Just finished unpacking them. What can you tell me about this lamp? I'm not sure I can keep it, Lamont." I didn't want to be angry with him, but I couldn't help myself.

"You saw what I saw, then. I don't know what to do with it. I really don't. It's a ghost light," Lamont confessed too easily.

"A ghost light? Is this some kind of trick? Is it battery operated? What did you do to this thing? I'm not interested in trick lamps." I gritted my teeth.

"No, I haven't done anything. I found it on my back step one day. It freaked my son out. He won't come to work if it's here. I can't afford to lose my only employee. I hope you can move it. Or know how to dispose of it."

I rubbed my sweaty forehead with the back of my hand. "Why don't you dispose of it?"

Lamont paused, which wasn't like him. He was never the kind of guy who was at a loss for words. "I tried, Henri. It kept coming back."

"You're kidding me, right?"

"No. I wish I were. I did some research, though. It is a theater light. It's said that every theater has a ghost and to scare the ghosts away, you must leave a ghost light burning on the stage. Other people believe that ghost lights appease the ghosts and keep them from sabotaging the production. So, whether it's keeping them away or making them happy, that's the story. I'm pretty sure this particular lamp came from the Franklin Theater here in Deridder."

I shook my head. "What am I supposed to do with this? I don't know any more than you do, Lamont."

"Not true, Devecheaux. The whole paranormal world here on the Gulf Coast is talking about you and the store. People talk. People trust you. I trust you. Please, help me with this. If you can't do anything with it, I'll take it back. Maybe I'll throw it in the ocean. I don't know."

What should I do? Lamont and I weren't the best of friends, but he was clearly troubled. Clearly frightened. Damn. Detra Ann would kill me if she knew what I was about to agree to.

"I'll see what I can do, but if I can't figure out what's going on, I'm going to hold you to it. You'll have to take it back," I warned him.

"Thanks, Henri." Lamont breathed a sigh of relief and hung up the phone.

Well, here we go again. No, make that here *I* go again. This one would be on me. Not Aggie, not Detra Ann, not Phoenix. Just me.

Me and the ghost light.

Author's Note: A. E. Chewning

W*arning:* If you haven't read the book, don't read the following notes. You'll get a spoiler in this section, and I wouldn't want you to be mad at me before you ever even get into the story.

For those of you that have read the story, let me go ahead and say that Monica and I were just as surprised as you were as the story unfolded that one of the characters had to leave us.

Is it temporary or final?

Who knows, but for this particular story, it felt right to let Patrice's character go into the darkness and lose her to it. Sometimes in life, we have to let go of people whether we want to or not. I've always lived by the motto that people come into your life for a reason and others for just a season. Each person I've encountered in my life has taught me lessons that I wouldn't have learned otherwise.

Deep, I know.

Aggie, no doubt, will gain strength in her loss. She will find herself through the pain and grow into who she is called to be. Losing special people in our lives sometimes forces us to evaluate what is truly important to us. We are led down a path to discover what we want in our own lives or who we want and need to become because of their absence.

Monica has gently pushed me into the idea of having Aggie and Phoenix branch off into their own series. Her intuition is impeccable, and I trust it. Honestly, when she first suggested it, I was a little worried and scared to death.

What if I can't do it alone?

As some of you know, or maybe some don't, I've written a trilogy and have started a series on my own before Monica and I collaborated on Devecheaux Antiques and Haunted Things. Neither of them has taken off as quickly as this one, but I enjoy those characters and stories and continue to develop them, hoping that one day they will.

I'm a newbie author. I fight imposter syndrome daily, sometimes hourly. It comes with the territory. But with my mentor and friend pushing me outside of my comfort zone and cheering me on, I've decided that I'll take that leap of faith and venture out into the unknown.

It will be fun. Right?

I'm hoping to launch the Society of the Supernatural series soon with their first case and investigation of the Houston Manor. The story is inspired by a house that sits across the street from my own. I see it every day while writing at my desk, and it's already been featured in a book about haunted locations in our area. Many volunteers have shared their personal stories of paranormal occurrences within the house. It's actually part of our local haunted walking tour.

Maybe the volunteers would let me sit over there for a Facebook Live.

Wouldn't that be interesting?

Thanks again for all of your support and kind words.

Until next time...

Happy reading,

A. E.

Author's Note: M.L. Bullock

And she's finished! *The Ghost Mirror*, Book Four in the Devecheaux Antiques and Haunted Things series, is the culmination of hours of brainstorming and pounding keyboards, but Ashley and I are pleased with the results. I hope you are too, despite the crushing ending. It's always hard letting go of a character, but sometimes tragedy is required to move the other characters along or to bring a new tension to the story.

We have two more books planned for this series, both of which will be equally exciting and will launch Aggie into the Seven Sisters world all by herself. Well, probably with Phoenix by her side, but who can say? On this point, I'll leave it up to Ashley. She has big plans for Phoenix and Aggie, and I can't wait to read all about it.

Writing *The Ghost Mirror* took a bit of time for me. I had some health issues—I think we can all agree that 2021 was hard on everyone. But I also took some time off to rest my tired brain. I can't believe it, but I've written over one hundred and forty books. Can you believe that? Seven Sisters and all her spin-offs. The Gulf Coast Paranormal series and *The Belles of Desire, Mississippi*, and so many others. I'm not stopping there. I've had the privilege of exploring new haunted places with a ton of new friends. (Shout out to Donna, Nichole, Joan and Nikki!)

Mobile, Alabama, has always been a favorite destination of mine. I lived in Mobile for decades, and honestly, it feels like home to me. From Bienville Square to Valhalla Cemetery, Mobile grabs my heart. It keeps me exploring. It keeps me connected to the amazing history of the South, the good and the bad. But there are tons of other places to see and feel and write about. My sweetheart and I plan on taking the Natchez Trace tour this spring. It's been on my bucket list for quite a long time.

Back to *The Ghost Mirror*. What a haunting, right? Mirrors are thought to be portals, windows to another dimension. Perhaps a ghost dimension. I've written about them before, but it's such a rich subject. How could we say no? And the idea of vampires in Mobile? Loved it! Typically, fiction writers think of New Orleans as the place for vampires, but Mobile is equally old, equally mystical. It's a forgotten gem to some people.

I love the Port City. It's a wonderful place. It's full of paranormal stories, legends and, of course, lots of ghost stories.

Thank you for reading *The Ghost Mirror*. Thank you for reading my books, Ashley's books and our collaborations. Please stay in touch. Follow me on Facebook[1] and be sure and sign up for my newsletter[2]. I send out a newsletter a few times a month, just to keep you posted on book sales, backstories and other cool things.

All my best,

M.L. Bullock

---

1. https://www.facebook.com/AuthorMLBullock
2. http://www.mlbullock.com

Don't miss out!

Visit the website below and you can sign up to receive emails whenever M.L. Bullock publishes a new book. There's no charge and no obligation.

https://books2read.com/r/B-A-CXMC-WVHDF

BOOKS 2 READ

Connecting independent readers to independent writers.

Also by M.L. Bullock

Create and Prosper
The Prolific Writer: How to Write and Create a Successful Catalog of Books

Delta Hex
The Devil's Bayou

Desert Queen Saga
The Tale of Nefret
The Falcon Rises
The Kingdom of Nefertiti
The Song of the Bee Eater

Devecheaux Antiques and Haunted Things
The Ghost Mirror

Devecheaux Antiques and Haunted Things Trilogy Series

Devecheaux Antiques and Haunted Things

A Cup of Shadows

A Voice From Her Past

A Watch Of Weeping Angels

Gulf Coast Paranormal

The Ghosts of Kali Oka Road

The Ghosts of the Crescent Theater

A Haunting on Bloodgood Row

The Legend of the Ghost Queen

A Haunting at Dixie House

The Ghost Lights of Forrest Field

The Ghost of Gabrielle Bonet

The Ghost of Harrington Farm

The Creature on Crenshaw Road

A Ghostly Ride in Gulfport

The Ghosts of Phoenix No.7

The Maelstrom of the Leaf Academy

The Ghosts of Oakleigh House

The Spirits of Brady Hall

The Gray Lady of Wilmer

Gulf Coast Paranormal Season Three

Tower of Darkness

Haunted Molly
Dead Children's Playground

Gulf Coast Paranormal Season Two
The Wayland Manor Haunting
The Beast of Limerick House
The Beast of Limerick House
A Haunting at Goliath Cave
Death Among the Roses
The Captain of Water Street
Return to the Leaf Academy

Gulf Coast Paranormal Trilogy Series
Ghosted
Haunted
Dead
Spooked
Paranormal

Haunting Passions
For the Love of Shadows
Her Haunted Heart

Idlewood

The Ghosts of Idlewood
Dreams of Idlewood
The Whispering Saint
The Haunted Child

Laurel House
Whispers

Lost Camelot
Guinevere Unconquered
The Undead Queen of Camelot

Lost Camelot Trilogy
Guinevere Forever

Marietta
The Bones of Marietta
Footsteps of Angels

Morgans Rock
The Haunting of Joanna Storm
The Hall of Shadows

The Ghost of Joanna Storm

Return to Seven Sisters

The Roses of Mobile

All the Summer Roses

Blooms Torn Asunder

A Garden of Thorns

Wreath of Roses

River Run

River Run

Rose Falls

Rose Falls

Rose Shadows

Rose Rising

Scary Fall Stories

Horrible Little Things

Seven Sisters

Seven Sisters

Moonlight Falls On Seven Sisters
Shadows Stir At Seven Sisters
The Stars That Fell
The Stars We Walked Upon
The Sun Rises Over Seven Sisters
Beyond Seven Sister
Ghost on a Swing

Shabby Hearts
A Touch Of Shabby
Shabbier By The Minute
Shabby By Night
Shabby All The Way
Star Spangled Shabby

Southern Gothic
Being With Beau
Death's Last Darling
Spook House

Southland
Southland

Sugar Hill

Wife Of The Left Hand
Fire On The Ramparts
Blood By Candlelight
The Starlight Ball
His Lovely Garden

Summerleigh
The Belles of Desire, Mississippi
The Ghost Of Jeoprady Belle
The Lady In White
Loxley Belle

Supernatural Support Group
Circle of Shadows

The Mummy Queen's Revenge
Queen Mummy

The Vampires of Rock and Roll
Elegant Black
Elegant Death

Twelve to Midnight

Mary Twelves

Standalone

The Hauntings of Idlewood

Lost Camelot

The Desert Queen Collection

Haunting Passions

Ghosts on a Plane

Halloween Screams

Dead Is the Loneliest Place to Be

Ghost Story

Believer's Guide to Paranormal Ministry

Haunted Chronicles of the Leaf Academy

Haunting Paranormal

Falls the Shadow

The Mourning Heart

Marietta

Watch for more at www.mlbullock.com.

About the Author

Author M.L. Bullock enjoys the laid-back atmosphere and the spooky vibe of the Gulf Coast, especially the region's historic districts and sites. When she isn't visiting her favorite haunts in New Orleans or Old Mobile, you can find her flipping through old photographs or newspaper clippings in search of new inspiration.

Read more at www.mlbullock.com.

